GREENMAIL

****

A. M. KEENE

BIXTER BOOKS / NEW YORK / 1986

GREENMAIL

PROLOGUE

Tuesday, February 18, 1986

Dow Jones News Service, 9:30 AM.

The New York Stock Exchange has announced that the stock of the United States Oil Company (USOCO) will not open this morning pending the release of a statement by the company.

It is widely presumed that the statement will concern recent takeover attempts of the company by foreign investors.

USOCO has been the subject of takeover speculation for the past six months, during which time the price of the stock rose from approximately $30 per share to $56 per share. USOCO stock closed on Friday, just before the Washington's Birthday weekend, at its high for the year.....

CHAPTER ONE

July, 1985

On this particular Wednesday morning, Matthew Allyn awoke earlier than usual, sweating profusely. The central air conditioning was on the blink again. He glanced over at the clock: 5:45 AM. He decided to make an early start for the office rather than stay in his high rise hot-box.

Forty-five minutes later, he entered the Lexington Avenue subway at 59th Street. Despite the early hour, it was not an improvement. It was hard to believe that in 1985, air conditioning still eluded the New York City transit system. Still, for a buck, it beat a $10 taxi ride downtown, which, considering the state of the stock market for the past six months, was now a lot of money to Matt for simple transportation.

Thirty-five long minutes later, the IRT Express arrived at the Wall Street stop. Matt headed up into the Irving Trust Building for a shoeshine giving Matt a chance to relax and read the Daily News without embarrassment.

Matt was well liked in the shoe shine parlor, because he was a consistent $1 tipper. He always marvelled at the various bankers and lawyers sharing the shoeshine bench. Dressed in three piece suits in the middle of a hot, humid New York summer, they carefully counted out their tips in nickels and dimes, much to the disdain of the shoe shine men.

Exiting on Broadway, Matt turned right onto Wall Street and walked down to #38, where a small suite of offices in the back of the eleventh floor housed the brokerage firm of Matthew Allyn and Company Inc. Entering the coffee shop on the ground floor, Matt decided on his version of a health food breakfast -- cornflakes and iced coffee to go. Taking the elevator up to the eleventh floor, Matt turned left and walked down to the end of the hall. He stooped down to pick up that day's "pink sheets", the over - the - counter quote sheets, left there by the early delivery. He glanced inside and saw that his own OTC stocks were down in price. So far the day had little positive to its credit.

Matt managed to unlock the door without spilling the coffee. The office was still dark except for the green glow of the quote machines' screens. He flipped on the lights and immediately checked the telex for messages or orders from his European clients. Today, as was the case for the past few months, the telex had remained silent all night. No orders, no business, not even any complaints. Wall Street brokerage is a feast or famine business -- and this was definitely famine.

Just then the phone rang. "Jesus!" thought Matt. "The damn thing actually works." He picked up the receiver and said in his most professional tone, "Matthew Allyn and Company. Can I help you?"

"Sure can. Any help you can give me will do." Matt laughed. It was his partner, Ted Whitehill, who handled the trading on the floor of the New York Stock Exchange. They'd been together for five years -- Whitey developed the domestic institutional business -- it was Matt's job to bring in the European banks.

"Well, we don't need help here -- it looks like another

3

dead day. You might as well go back to sleep. You don't have to be on the floor till ten o'clock anyway."

"Uh, well, I'm here with Ann." Whitey had described Ann to Matt as a "killer barracuda -- a real eat'em alive" type. But then, Whitey had a tendency to complain about all his girlfriends, no matter what their personal qualities. None of them had seemed able to make him happy since his divorce two years ago.

"Sounds like a personal problem to me," said Matt, jokingly. Then he picked up on Whitey's hint. "Why don't you come downtown early anyway. I need you to help me plan my trip to Europe."

"OK. If you need me, I'll be down in a few minutes," said Whitey. Although he rarely got involved with Matt's business trips, he was clearly pleased to have an excuse to leave Ann's apartment before any early morning demands were put on him.

Matt's mind wandered back to the first couple of years. He and Whitey had struggled hard to develop a customer base. It wasn't easy. The firm did not produce any of Wall Street's typical research reports which could be sold to institutional customers in return for commission dollars generated by their stock brokerage transactions. Instead, he and Whitey focused their sales pitch on their ability to act as ferrets on the floor of the Stock Exchange -- gleaning information about who was doing what to whom in which stock and other tidbits that the large brokerage houses did not really pass along. Matt and Whitey had succeeded in a small way -- they were making a living, but not "knocking 'em dead."

Matt started reviewing his notes of his last trip to Europe six months ago. He managed to generate a few more firms interest, but did not land any big accounts. You are never told in management training about the misery of a slow market -- and wisely, reasoned Matt.

The door to the office opened. Whitey, looking unusually tired, walked in and slumped down in the chair next to him. Matt looked over at Whitey. At 44 years of age, Whitey looked older than he should, partly due to twenty years on the floor of the New York Stock Exchange. Being a floor broker more closely resembles manual labor than most people think. Trades are executed at the post of the specialist handling a particular stock. Getting around to the various posts is done solely by footpower -- and the Exchange's physical plant is huge. Sore feet and fallen arches are the profession's biggest medical problems.

"Jeez, Whitey. You look like dead meat. Here, have some of my coffee."

"You say the nicest things, Matt." Whitey downed the coffee and stretched his limbs. Matt knew that that gesture was his signal that he wanted to only discuss business. Must have been a less than perfect evening. "Anything in the Journal that I should know about?"

"Well, the big Wall Street whiz kids are looking for the summer rally to begin any time now."

"Oh, swell." The market generally does the exact opposite of what is predicted, especially if the prediction is made by a 'market guru'. "Well, then that's the kiss of death for sure." Whitey frowned. "Shit, I'm so ready for a rally, too. These bear markets are the fucking pits."

Matt felt the same way. Even with all their combined years as stockbrokers, they still were unable to deal with the boredom of a dead market. Depending on the immediate outlook for the Dow, their personal emotions ranged from general itchiness to an out and out what - the - hell - am - I -

5

doing - in - this - fucking - business funk. Right then both were closer to the latter feeling than they were willing to admit to each other.

Matt tried to calm Whitey. "Well, there's nothing we can do about it here. I think I'll take off for Europe next week and see if I can't turn up something over there."

"Where are you planning on going?" asked Whitey.

"First stop Dusseldorf. Horst has invited me for the weekend and he hinted at some new contacts for me to meet. After Dusseldorf, I'll push on to Switzerland and play it by ear from there."

"Sounds okay, but I hope it works a little better than the last trip."

Matt grimaced. "Hey, Whitey, it takes time for things to happen. You just don't have lunch with someone and get handed an order to buy 100,000 IBM over strudel and coffee. I'm not telling you anything you don't know. You've known the Morgan Stanley broker on the floor for over ten years and I haven't seen you execute a 1000 shares of anything for them in all that time."

"Yeah, okay. You're right. And when you're right, you're right." Whitey wasn't up to arguing in his hungover state, but he was just as anxious as Matt to get more business in the door.

It was edging on to 9:00 AM and the firm's staff had begun filtering in. Last in was Jerry Stern, Matt's assistant. A John Travolta look-alike from Brooklyn, he gathered a lot of attention from the female sales assistants and secretaries in the office, which tended to make him a little cocky, in the broadest sense of the word.

Matt looked at his watch -- 9:10. "Morning, Jerry," deadpanned Matt. "Thanks for showing up."

"Gimme a break, Matt. I don't see any time clocks here -- or is it buried under the pile of orders from Europe."

Matt grimaced. He knew that in normal times this sarcasm would have been all part of the morning's give-and-take. But in slow times, such comments were less welcome. The mood in the office was definitely beginning to sour.

Matt turned, picked up the telephone and called Lufthansa reservations.

CHAPTER TWO

After the close of trading the following Friday afternoon, Matt found himself mired in traffic in the Queens Midtown Tunnel on his way to JFK Airport. He had reserved a coach seat -- business class was full and first class too expensive -- on the 6:30 Lufthansa flight to Dusseldorf. As he sat in the cab he attempted to switch his mind to the next few days awaiting him. Horst always entertained well -- generally including the company of fine German frauleins. It would be a welcome relief from the tedium of the last few weeks in New York.

An hour later than usual they arrived at the Lufthansa gate. He rushed to the counter to check his bags and arrange his seat, and ran to the gate -- only to find that the flight would be delayed forty five minutes. Fucking summer tourists, he thought, do they all have to go to Europe tonight?

With time on his hands until the boarding call, he pulled out the latest issue of Forbes. The magazine's cover had a cleverly crafted illustration of gushing oilwells drilling, not on the Texas panhandle, but on Wall Street. But instead of spewing oil, they were spewing dollar bills. The article focused on the latest mania in financial circles -- the mega buck mergers in the oil industry.

Starting in 1981, CONOCO was swallowed by DuPont. Soon after, Marathon Oil was acquired by U.S. Steel, Cities Service by Occidental Petroleum, Getty by Texaco, Superior Oil by Mobil and Gulf Oil by Standard Oil of California. The list continues. By now anything was possible. The large money center banks were lending feverishly to the takeover raiders in order to replenish the loans lost in the debacle of third world debt rescheduling.

Who would be next was anyone's guess -- speculation centered on such tempting domestic targets as Amerada Hess and Sun Oil. Only the real giants, like Exxon, Mobil and USOCO, seemed immune. The vast sums necessary to acquire one of those companies would be beyond the reach of even the largest lending consortium. Besides, it would take an immense ego for any individual to even begin to think of such an attempt.

"Now boarding Lufthansa flight 206 to Dusseldorf."

The sudden announcement jarred Matt out of his reverie. He picked up his attache case and made his way for the gate. The gathering mob of summer tourists guaranteed a noisy, exhausting flight. Matt's survival technique consisted of a couple of bottles of California Chardonnay and classical music on the headphones -- not exactly ideal but the best he could do.

Eight hours later, the miserable flight now a memory, Matt registered at the Muench Hotel, on the Koenigsallee, or 'the Ko', as the locals referred to it. Matt loved it there. It had a fabulous old world charm, and belonged to that fast-vanishing breed -- a family run hotel. It was far removed from the sterilty of the modern Hilton near the airport. He treated himself to a hot bath and a couple of hours sleep before Horst would pick him up for lunch.

9

Feeling much refreshed a few hours later, Matt sauntered down to the lobby of the hotel and sat down in one of the large red leather chairs off to its side. He ordered a Campari and soda, and as it arrived so did Horst. He looked as elegant as always. Tall with slightly graying hair, a full mustache on top of a strong chin, he looked every bit the part of an urbane European banker.

Horst Meyer was the senior partner of Bankhaus J. Meyer & Sohne, a small bank in Dusseldorf run by his father. He also happened to be Matt's best customer in Europe. Matt and Horst had been roommates almost fifteen years earlier when both were students at the University of Geneva. But Horst's future had always been secure at his father's bank, while Matt had to make it on his own. But contacts are the name of the brokerage game and Horst had always been a fervent supporter of Matt's efforts to extend his scope of business in Europe. If Horst had someone for Matt to meet it had a good chance of being productive.

"Wie geht's, Matt."

"Ganz gut. Was gibt's."

The two had said hello to each other in the same way since their university days. It was a signal that all was okay.

"It's wonderful to see you again, Matt. Come on, drink up. I've made special plans for lunch and we're running late."

Matt downed the drink -- the bittersweet flavor of the Campari giving him the lift he needed.

"Where are we going? We've got a lot to talk about."

"To my club outside town. I've invited a Swiss banker that I thought you should meet."

Matt's spirits were steadily improving. Horst was coming through for him. It was great to have friends, mused Matt, and even better to have well connected ones.

They got into the Horst's Mercedes and proceeded to his hunt club, which was just below the Jaegerhof Castle, an old hunting lodge constructed in the 18th Century. It was designed along the same lines, and was set amidst large oak trees and well-maintained country roads. It took Matt back in time to another more elegant era. The club was renowned for its annual fox hunt, but Horst, a bachelor, had used it mainly as a place to entertain bankers and other guests.

"How's it going at the bank?" asked Matt on the way there.

"Good. Good." Horst sounded unenthusiastic.

Matt picked up on the inuendo. "But not great."

"Oh, everything's fine. It's just that my father's in such control that it hard to do anything on my own. I'm in charge of the bank's investments, but it's only a title. Everything must pass under his nose before it can be approved. Mostly he's right -- but it's so damn constraining."

"Can't you ask him for more authority?"

"I have." Horst's voice rose a bit. Matt had evidently touched on an exposed nerve. "Many times. Many, many times."

"Won't he be retiring soon?"

"Him. He's as healthy as a horse. He'll never give up. Besides he loves to tell me that I am wrong -- I can see it in his face. I think my mistakes keep him going."

11

"But you must be right sometimes."

"Of course, I'm right sometimes. But then he never gives me credit for it. He says that he thought of it first. I would have to do something very big on my own in order to prove myself." Horst was becoming very agitated. Matt decided to remain quiet for a while.

After a few minutes, Horst calmed down. "You know, Matt, you are very lucky to have your own company. Then you can do as you like."

"Lucky? I guess. But we are not making money like you are. We are still a little piss-ant outfit."

"Don't worry. You'll get bigger. Maybe my guest can help."

"Who is this guest?"

"You'll see."

When they arrived, Horst parked next to a larger, white Mercedes with Swiss license plates that revealed the owner to be from Geneva. "Andre must already be here," he stated. Matt felt that Horst was being just a bit secretive about who the guest was -- he hoped it was worth all the game playing.

Horst escorted him to the dining area. The interior was resplendent with half timbering and stag's heads -- simultaneously evincing in Matt a feeling of delight and repugnance -- hunting was not a sport that he tolerated well. Near the long oak bar that preceded the entrance to the main dining room stood someone who appeared to Matt as a blond version of Horst -- slightly taller, no mustache, but the same elegance of bearing that Matt associated with wealth. Horst walked Matt in his direction.

12

"Matt, I would like you to meet Andre LeFevre. Andre, this is Matt Allyn, my most competent stockbroker."

Matt now understood the touch of secrecy. Horst wanted to surprise him with this introduction to the owner of one of Switzerland's most prestigious private banks -- an introduction that he knew Matt would truly savor. Horst was right. Matt had never succeeded in even arranging a meeting at LeFevre & Cie. Matt almost flubbed his response, he was so taken.

"*Enchante,*" replied Andre, obviously a French speaking Swiss, which added to his cosmopolitan air. Matt eyed him more closely. He was attired in a double breasted navy blue sport coat, a blue shirt with a white collar, a red striped tie. A paisley handkerchief was stuffed in the jacket's pocket so casually as to be half falling out -- which Matt recognized as a deliberate sign of insouciance on the part of self-confident Europeans.

The language had switched to English, in which both Horst and Andre were fluent. Andre had been summarizing his drive up to Germany to Horst. Horst listened attentively. He, too, was obviously impressed with Andre's presence. "But I am really starved," Andre was saying. "May we eat?"

The three were seated near a corner window, which had an excellent view of the corral. For a few minutes, they watched various riders go through their paces. Matt was amused to see that the Germans took their riding almost as seriously as the British -- and with slightly more formality, if that seemed possible.

"I have taken up riding as a hobby. In fact, I recently bought a quarterhorse of my own. I'll show you Lars later," Horst said, referring to his own mount at the stable. "He is really developing into a fine jumper -- and so am I. I'm

13

thinking seriously of signing up for the annual foxhunt next February."

Matt, who was never trained in horsemanship, and couldn't stand the jerkiness of the ride, was pleased when the conversation switched to a far more comfortable topic, the stock market. Andre was surprisingly attentive. Matt had presumed that Andre would ask the perfunctory questions, but Andre was apparently sincerely interested in Matt's comments. He hoped that Horst had not overly built up his capabilities to Andre -- it might only serve to make a fool of him in the long run.

"Tell me about these oil takeovers," asked Andre. "Many of my clients wonder why I am not more active in them -- they seem to feel that it is a guaranteed way to double their money."

Matt smiled. He knew what Andre meant. For every one indiviual who did well by takeovers, there were two who were heavily burned when a deal fell through.

"Well, the market is ripe for anything with glamour. The rise in the Dow Jones Index between 1982 and 1983 whetted everyone's appetite for making money in the market again -- and they want to keep that feeling despite the market's decline during the last couple of years. So rather than spreading their money around the market in bits and pieces, people are betting big bucks on takeover rumors. The oils have definitely been the most fertile patch."

"But wouldn't you wait for some assurance of a takeover before you placed your bets."

"No, no. By then it would be too late. The trick is to guess which are the next likely acquisitions. Even unfounded rumors are good ways to make money. For instance, if a company is the butt of rumor campaign, people

14

will rush in to buy the stock, causing the price to rise whether or not the rumor is founded. Big money can be made -- but only if you are sharp enough to get out before the rumor is exposed and the stock collapses." Matt wondered if he was sounding too pretentious.

"What about those stocks that are bid up by one buyer, who then makes a tender offer to buy the whole company? But rather than be owned by that buyer the company buys off the buyer, at a much higher price than he paid."

Matt laughed out loud. Sitting in an old lodge eating roast duck with spaetzle made many of the Wall Street machinations seem ludicrous. Besides, his spirits were constantly rising.

"That, my friend, is what is now known as 'Greenmail', which are financial manipulations done by so-called 'Wall Street Robin Hoods'. It is a way of legally redistributing the wealth of the country. But unlike the real Robin Hood, who stole from the rich and gave it to the poor, they take from wealthy companies and keep it for themselves."

They all laughed. Another bottle of wine was ordered. Matt was clearly making a good impression and he drank heartily.

After lunch they took a tour of the grounds. Horst took them to the stable where he kept his tack and the various guns used for the small game hunts. Each member had his own box, which were stacked neatly near the tackmaster's office.

"Herr Barnum," Horst said. "Would you open my box -- I wish to take Lars out for a ride." The German dutifully obliged. Matt noted that the tackmaster in his outfit looked every bit like the circus ringmaster that his name connoted. Were everything not handled so seriously, Matt would have probably laughed at the tendency towards pompousness. Horst removed a saddle and bridle, which were beautifully polished. Inside the box Matt noticed some rifles and a gun, which were also highly polished. Herr Barnum must do his job well, thought Matt.

The stablehand brought out Lars, a tall, handsome thoroughbred with very deep chestnut coloring. Horst put Lars through several paces in the outdoor corral, including a number of jumps over a brick wall. Matt and Andre applauded the show from the sidelines. After the demonstration, Horst continued walking Lars around the course to cool him off. Andre turned suddenly toward Matt.

"Do your plans for next week include Geneva?"

"Yes," said Matt. Even if they hadn't, he would have put them in.

"In that case, you must come and visit our bank. I'll be there all week and I'll arrange for you to meet our head trader, Raoul Hengler."

"My pleasure," said Matt, revealing only about half the emotion he felt. Looking out at Horst calmly pacing Lars on the beautifully kept grounds, hearing Andre offer him the most promising chance in months, Matt felt as far removed from the dreariness of New York as he ever would.

They stayed at the club until 3 o'clock, then Horst drove Matt back to town. They made arrangements to meet at a supper club in the *Altstatd* at 9 o'clock -- Horst said that he would provide the 'entertainment'. Horst showed up a half hour late, with two females on his arms, Ursala and Mitzi, both dressed in leather outfits, carrying large leather bags.

They said they were secretaries, but their slightly too much make-up and decidely too-little clothes gave away their true profession.

Matt didn't care. Horst had obviously been with them before. They seemed to have their own routines -- they joked in German and broken English. Matt was laughing even harder than Horst because it had been so long since he had been in good spirits. The evening ended at Horst's apartment, where the girls got down to 'business'. Matt landed up with Mitzi, because Horst had chosen Ursala, whose black leather pants had attracted Horst's attention all night. Matt didn't care --neither girl, for all their efforts, appealed to him sexually -- he would have been just as pleased if the evening had ended after dinner. In any case, Mitzi proved competent in her trade and ultimately Matt felt that he had not wasted Horst's money.

Not that he thought that Horst would have cared. Matt figured that Horst used Matt's visit as an excuse to indulge his own fantasies -- as he was leaving Horst's apartment, Mitzi went in to join the other two. She carried her bag in with her -- Matt figured that it contained more exotic paraphenalia then his own sexual needs required.

The next day Matt decided to see the city on foot and left right after lunch. When he arrived back at the hotel at 5:00, there was a message that Horst had called at 2:00. Matt tried to return the call but there was no answer. Matt was relieved -- it would have been too uncomfortable to have to rehash the previous night. He would call again after he returned to New York.

CHAPTER THREE

Having completed several perfunctory business calls by Wednesday with other potential clients in Germany, Matt caught a midmorning Swissair flight to Geneva. The allure of Andre's invitation had preoccupied his thinking and his imagination was going full tilt with the anticipation of a possible business relationship with LeFevre & Cie.

In this state of excitation, Matt barely noticed the heavy thud of the wheels on the runway as the flight landed in Geneva's perennially cloud-covered Cointrin airport. Despite the midsummer date, Geneva was cool and damp, giving Matt a chill as he grabbed a cab.

"Hotel du Rhone, s'il vous plait." Matt preferred speaking French to German -- already he was feeling much more comfortable by just being in Geneva.

"Oui, d'accord. As you wish, M'sieur."

It took about twenty five minutes for the cab to pull up to the entrance to the hotel on the Quai Turrettini overlooking the Rhone River. The hotel was not one of Matt's favorites. The corridors reminded him of a ship's passageways curving around within the structure of the hotel. His room was like a small stateroom -- a tiny single bed with hardly any space to maneuver. But it was only a short walk to 68 Rue du Mont

Blanc, where LeFevre & Cie was situated.

After a quick shower and change of clothes, Matt left the
hotel and proceeded to his appointment with Andre. LeFevre
& Cie. was housed in a typical Geneva building. It was an
imposing structure, faced with a large gray-green cut stone
facade and leaded windows. Like a fortress, the interior was
heavily protected from the intrusion of the outside world. On
a brass plate near the entry were the letters "LF&C" -- the
only indication of the company's name. Casual visitors were
clearly not invited. Entering through a solid oak door, his
foot steps sounded loudly on the marble floor as he
approached the guard seated at the desk directly ahead.

"Matthew Allyn to see Monseiur LeFevre."

"One moment, please," said the guard as he rang
LeFevre's office. "Monsieur LeFevre's secretary will be
down shortly, sir."

Matt paced the length of the lobby as he waited. Along
the wall hung the photographs of the former directors of the
bank, stretching back four generations. The bank had been
founded in the late 1870's by Marc Justin LeFevre, Andre's
great grandfather. He had made millions as a dealer,
supplying Swiss made armaments to both sides during the
Franco-Prussian War. These war profits enabled Marc
LeFevre to gain respectability in society for his descendants
who would be known as bankers, not as arms dealers.

Just then the small elevator behind Matt opened. As Matt
turned, he heard a charming voice say, "Monsieur Allyn.
Good afternoon. I'm Christine Evins, secretary to Monsieur
LeFevre."

Matt was accoustomed to seeing beautiful women in
New York on every corner, but Christine Evins was
spectacular. Tall, with shapely legs, and a fine boned face

capped with shoulder length honey blond hair, she was truly a vision.

She wore a simple blue chemise dress with white collar and cuffs, with a single strand of pearls as the only accessory. On many women the look would have been too stark, but she carried it off with the grace and elegance of a designer's model.

As he followed her into the elevator, he found it difficult to concentrate on his upcoming meeting. A faint trace of jasmine based perfume filled the air.

"I hope you're having a good trip, Monsieur Allyn," said Christine.

He thought to himself that the best part of the trip had just begun, but said politely, "Yes, very nice, thank you."

The elevator arrived at the third floor, and Christine led him down the thickly carpeted hall to Andre's large corner office.

"Here we are, Monsieur Allyn," leading him into a high ceiling office resplendent with French decor.

"Thank you, Mademoiselle Evins. It was delightful to meet you." He was pleased that she did not correct his usage of the term Madamoiselle, and assumed that she must be, if not unattached, at least single.

"Matt, how are you. It's good to see you again." Andre's strong voice reverberated from behind a Louis Quinze desk.

"Andre, I'm very happy to be here."

"Please have a seat. Would you care for some coffee --

or perhaps something stronger?"

"No, coffee will be just fine, thank you," said Matt, as he sat down in a soft, plush fauteuil. As Andre relayed the order to Christine through the intercom, Matt observed the office which had more the ambiance of a French chateau than that of a bank. There was an exquisite Aubusson rug covering the parquet floor, art reminiscent of Watteau on the walls and a bas relief ceiling. Matt wondered which of the LeFevres were inspired to decorate in this style.

"You know, Matt, you're not the first broker to sit in this office. They all come to see me -- the Morgan Stanley's, the Merrill's, the First Boston's. But they all have the same thing to say. It's like hearing a broken record. 'Give us your business,' they say, 'we'll give you the best research available, and you'll make a lot of money for youself and your clients.' "

Andre moved to the front of the antique desk and sat on the edge, as if to disregard its age. The whole effect seemed slightly staged to Matt, who was sure that Andre probably took that position many times as a way of subtle intimidation of any visitor.

"But you know, Matt it's not like that. By the time their advice reaches Europe, it is already old news. It might as well have come on a slow steamer across the Atlantic.

"Would you like to know the result of their investment advice over the past few years? Let me tell you. It always turns out that we buy on the top and sell on the bottom. Even our own investment banker in New York, Hillman Flax, has been mediocre at best."

It was as if Andre was deliberately giving Matt the perfect cue for his sales pitch.

21

"Andre, that's why Matthew Allyn and Company is in business. We have no axe to grind. Our business does not depend on selling the customer research. We are specialists in executing large orders well and in keeping the customers plugged into what's happening on the floor of the New York Stock Exchange.

"We think that this differentiates us from the firms you mentioned. You know that for many large brokers their domestic clients are more important to them than some one such as yourself. That's not the case with us."

"Well, Matt, that sounds good, but I believe that brokers are always prone to exaggerate." Andre's comment let some of the air out of Matt's balloon -- he thought the sell had gone a little too smoothly.

Andre continued, "Nevertheless, Matt, you have a good reputation with Horst -- and Horst is a good friend of mine. I've known him for many years. It might be possible for us to work together. But let's talk about that later.

"First, come with me -- I'd like to take you to our trading room and introduce you to Raoul Hengler who's in charge of that department."

The trading room, which was located below ground level, was a complete anomaly compared to the two hundred year old structure in which it was housed. The far end of the room had a large screen on which was projected the Reuters News Service, foreign exchange quotes, gold and commodity prices and the New York Stock Exchange ticker tape. Seated around a horseshoe trading desk were six traders, each charged with a certain area of responsibility -- the U.S., U.K., Swiss, West German, Tokyo and the other world stock markets were individually covered. In front of each of them were state-of-the-art commmunication systems. Behind them clerks were in constant motion, logging trades and balancing positions. In a small glass walled office off to the side, the senior trader, Raoul Hengler, oversaw the whole operation.

Matt mentally estimated the cost of the physical set-up, which had to have been well over a million for the equipment alone. It made his own office's trading desk look quite primitive by comparison.

"Raoul, I'd like to introduce Mr. Matthew Allyn, the stockbroker from New York that Horst Meyer recommended to us."

"I'm very happy to meet you," said Raoul in thickly accented English. Short, stocky and dark, Raoul was Andre's physical antithesis. Heavy horn rimmed glasses magnified eyes which darted around the room, as if constantly checking for problems.

"My pleasure," said Matt, quite sincerely. "You have quite a trading desk here."

"It works well, but only because I have some talented people."

"Are your traders active in U.S. stocks?"

"Well, the Arabs seem to be especially fond of the U.S. market these days."

"Oh, are you doing much business with the Arabs?"

Raoul and Andre smiled at each other, as if there were some inside joke between them.

"Yes. In fact, quite a bit. Quite frankly, that's why we are looking for a new broker. We don't need the research from the big New York names -- these Arabs know exactly what they want to buy. They are looking for what they consider to be the perfect combination -- Swiss secrecy and American investments. That is where you come in. We are looking for a talented, but not overpriced, broker."

Matt understood a little more of what was going on. Or so he thought. The Swiss bank is now investing on behalf of Middle Eastern interests. If they bought directly into stocks in the US, they might be subject to exposure or even an asset freeze if there was any trouble in the Middle East.

However, by using the Swiss as intermediaries, they keep their anonymity. Naturally, the Swiss get the benefit of their funds, and by using a small broker like Matt, get the attention and institutional pricing that the big brokers could not offer.

"I think I can offer you a competitive deal. If you are doing block trades, that is. Are you anticipating doing large transactions?"

Again, Andre and Raoul eyed each other.

"Yes, pretty much." Andre responded. "But, you know, whatever we do will require the utmost, uh, discretion on your part."

Matt responded eagerly. "Whatever the customer wants. We aim to please."

"Good, good. Then let's iron out some details."

Matt eagerly pulled out the account opening papers, and discussed the firm's pricing on large trades. He handed the package over to Andre, who passed them on to Raoul.

"We'll process these right away and forward them onto you. We'll do all our transactions by telex. Since this is

24

important to us, either Raoul or I will be the telex signatory. We'll give you a special telex number that goes right into Raoul's office. Use that solely."

"No problem. We're good at special handling."

"Excellent. You know, Matt, if you're half as good as Horst says, I think we'll make a lot of money together." Matt felt his body getting warmer. This was definitely a major breakthrough.

The sound of the opening door brought Matt back into reality. Christine entered carrying a tray of the almost forgotten coffee. The sight of her completed the perfection of the moment for Matt.

CHAPTER FOUR

At the end of the meeting, Raoul escorted Matt to the elevator while Andre returned to his office.

"No calls, Miss Evins," which Miss Evins always presumed to mean that LeFevre was about to take a few minutes' nap.

Instead, Andre closed the door to his office, pulled out a key from his pocket key chain, unlocked the credenza behind his desk, and retrieved a thick handwritten ledger.

Although Andre was quite familiar with the contents, he stared at the numbers for a long time. Finally, he picked up the phone and dialed Raoul's number on a line which was specially wired not to register at his secretary's desk.

"Well, Raoul, what did you think of our little stockbroker friend."

"He's perfect. Eager and naive."

"I agree. Let's get things rolling."

"We'll give him a week and then move."

"Good." Andre hung up the phone, returned the papers to the credenza, and buzzed the intercom.

"Miss Evins. I'm open for business again."

CHAPTER FIVE

Leaving LeFevre & Cie, Matt had a feeling of lightheadedness as he perceived a real breakthrough for himself and his firm. Since his schedule was clear for the rest of the afternoon and Geneva's weather had improved during Matt's meeting at the bank, he allowed the sun to warm his face as he strolled down the Rue du Mont Blanc towards Lac Leman. In the distance, he was able to see Mont Blanc itself, a rare occurance since it is usually hidden by clouds. He could also see Geneva's trademark, the Jet d'Eau, which rose majestically from a jetty out on the lake.

As he reached the lake, Matt decided to stop for a beer at Le Bateau, an old converted paddle steamer which was now a restaurant. As he drank, he mentally reenacted the day's events and thought of how he was going to relate the good news to Whitey. The whole process had gone very smoothly, too smoothly for just a cold call. Horst must have made it happen, he decided -- well, better lucky than smart.

As Matt pulled out his wallet to pay his bill, he looked up and saw Christine Evins walking intently towards the lake.

Without thinking, he called out in English, "Miss Evins, over here." Not very suave, he realized. He should have at least said it in French.

"Oh, Monsieur Allyn," she responded, somewhat taken aback.

"Did I startle you? I'm sorry, you were passing so quickly. Would you care to join me for a drink?"

"Oh, no, thank you, I really must run." Matt sensed that she was being coy. Undoubtedly, it was considered bad form to fraternize with customers.

"Not even one? I promise not to tell Andre. Besides it would be good for your company's business."

She hestitated for a moment. Clearly the excuse was weak, but it only needed to be adequate. "Well, in that case, I guess it would be all right." She slipped into the seat next to his at the small outdoor table, adjusting it so that it would be directly opposite him. "I'll have a lillet on ice, please."

Matt suddenly felt awkward and fumbled for something to say.

"Do you live nearby?"

"Yes, I have a small apartment near the English Gardens. It was left to me by my grandparents."

"Oh, you live by yourself, then?" asked Matt.

"Well, most of the time," Christine answered, thwarting his rather obvious question.

Matt shifted his tack. He knew the Swiss were very reserved and he undoubtedly was coming on too strong.

28

"I was very impressed with the LeFevre & Cie. organization. Have you been working there long?"

"Six years. I joined them after completing my Unversity training. I studied economics, but in Switzerland it is still very hard for a woman to get a professional job. But I speak English and German well, and I can type. So I am Mr. LeFevre's secretary."

Christine was opening up a little. Matt took the cue.

"I absolutely feel that in Europe women are an underdeveloped resource. In America we are much more appreciative of women's abilities." Christine smiled. Matt had obviously hit the right chord. "But are you unhappy with what you do?" he asked.

No one had ever asked Christine that question before. Certainly not another businessman. "Yes, I think I am. I would rather be doing something, eh, well, more important." Christine felt as if she were complaining, something one didn't do in Switzerland with strangers. "But some aspects I really enjoy. Such as dealing with the customers. I directly handle many of their little problems on behalf of Mr. LeFevre. I like the people and I like the variety."

"Are there many "little problems" at LeFevre?"

"Oh, no. In fact, the bank is doing very well. When the customers call they all tell me how pleased they are with their accounts."

"What do you think of Andre LeFevre?" Matt knew the question was a bit forward -- besides, he had already formed his own opinion of LeFevre. But he felt compelled to know if there was any relationship between Christine and her boss.

"Oh, he is quite, uh, intelligent." And handsome, and wealthy, and charming, added Matt mentally. Leave it alone, he decided, this is the wrong time and place. Change tacks again.

"Miss Evins, this has turned out to be such a lovely evening. Could I induce you to join me later for dinner?"

"Oh, I never have dinner with customers. It would not be right."

Matt had stepped over the line this time. He thought fast to save the situation.

"Ah, but, you know, I am really not a customer. I am a broker -- and LeFevre is my customer. And I always take customers to dinner. That our company's policy."

Christine looked at him. At first he had a serious look, but then a small grin spread over his face, revealing a seeming guilelessness. He was very different from the typically reserved Swiss men she had dated. Suddenly, she found herself charmed by his openness. "All right, but we must make it an early night. I have a lot of work in the office tomorrow."

Matt understood what she was telling him -- but the terms were perfectly acceptable. "I'll pick you up at eight."

"No, that's all right. I'll meet you at the restaurant."

"Very well. I'll make reservations at Le Parc des Eaux-Vives." One of Geneva's best restaurants and worth the occasion.

"*D'accord.* I'll see you then." She gave him a bright smile and left in the direction of the Gardens.

Later, as Matt was dressing, he surveyed himself in the mirror. How would he stack up against Andre? Younger? Decidedly. More attractive? No, not unless you liked wavy brown hair, brown eyes and soft features. Richer? Matt's fortune was still in the "all potential" stage. More charming? Matt couldn't compete on the "oozing continental charm" score. Should he aim for disarming over charming?

The restaurant displayed all the aspects of elegance that Matt required. Its gleaming crystal and delicate flowers set the stage for the perfect evening. Christine only added to the decor. She wore a indigo blue silk dress that set off her hair and eyes. Matt was instantly taken. Was it his imagination? Were European women naturally more elegant, more sophisticated? Did their formality and reserve only heighten their beauty? Or was it simply the different locale that made her seem more appealing?

They were seated in a relatively quiet spot towards the far wall. After they placed orders for drinks, Matt groped for conversation. He wanted to ask her a dozen questions about herself, but each seemed too direct. Nor was Christine easing the situation -- she was clearly only responding to his cues. Matt decided to stick to safe ground for a while.

"When did Andre LeFevre take over as Managing Director?"

"Five years ago, when Michel LeFevre died. I had only started then -- but the father was very fearsome. A booming voice and a strict rule. I could not have worked for him."

"So Andre was trained well at LeFevre."

31

"Yes, but old LeFevre ran everything. No one dared contradict him -- not even Monsieur LeFevre, Andre, that is."

So, Matt thought, she still calls him Monsieur. Should he derive any clues from that?

"So Andre suddenly had a free hand when Michel died. He must have relished that idea."

"Oh, yes. That is when he put in the new trading room and hired most of the traders. Up until then, LeFevre was quite conservative -- or so I'm told. Monsieur LeFevre, Andre, changed everything. They spread out their customers' funds all over the world and in all different types of investments."

"When did Raoul Hengler come in?"

"With the new trading room. He organized it, and the computer system to handle all the accounts."

"He sounds like quite a boon to the firm."

"Oh, yes. He works very hard. He stays late most every night."

Probably reading the material sent by all the market gurus. "Catching up on old news from the whiz kids?" he said sarcastically.

Christine didn't grasp the joke. "Oh, no. Doing the accounts. He double checks each one personally. He is very thorough."

Raoul was beginning to bore Matt. He hoped that he was not also competing against Raoul, although his coke bottle lenses and bookish ways would suggest otherwise.

"Do you ever come to New York?"

Christine stared intently at Matt. "Yes, sometimes," she said. And then she grinned. "The bank sends me," she added.

"Really. Do you handle customers there?"

"Well, yes. No, not exactly. I, uh, handle, uh, a very special customer."

This is the part Matt feared -- she must "handle" Andre. Matt knew that the Swiss were very discreet about what they did in their own country -- but on foreign soil they were as ready as anyone for the big game.

Christine caught his dejected look. "No, no. I know what you are thinking -- it's not that at all. At least, not on my part. I'll tell you sometime -- it's a bit of a, well, a secret." She laughed.

That had broken the ice for Matt. Right now he didn't care what "the secret" was -- she was laughing and ready to open up. Matt ordered another round of drinks and asked for the menus.

The rack of lamb persille was superb, but Matt barely noticed it. The conversation had moved swiftly -- they covered everything from his university days in Geneva to her girlhood romances. He explained about starting the firm, and the four years of patient growth. She appeared to be very interested.

"You know," she said, "in this country, you cannot start a company so easily. It must be handed down to you from

33

family to family. Being an entrepreneur is very difficult --
the business connections are very entrenched and the banks
will not lend you the money to start up anyway. I admire
you for attempting this."

Matt leaned back slowly. "You must come and see the
firm the next time you are in New York. But I must warn
you, the offices will not rival those of LeFevre & Cie."

"Yes, but it's your firm, and you don't have a hundred
years of history behind you, as LeFevre does."

Matt beamed. Did she mean it, or was that just part of
the European charm?

"It takes a long time to build a business -- I suspect it
may take a lifetime. But we have nothing else to do anyway,
so we might as well do that."

Christine laughed.

"Why did you laugh?" Matt asked. "It wasn't that funny
a joke."

"Oh no. It's just that you Americans are so much more
honest about themselves than we Swiss. You just say
whatever you are thinking. You are so much more enjoyable
than men who are constantly trying to impress me with their
achievements."

After Matt paid the check, he ventured another advance
with her. "Allow me to escort you home."

"No, no. I'll just take a taxi."

"Oh, but it's a beautiful evening. Let's walk along the
lake."

Ultimately, she allowed him to walk her all the way home. As she placed the key in the apartment door she bade him good-night. Clearly, she was not inviting him in. Matt himself did not wish to sully the evening with any unwelcome gestures. Everything had gone too smoothly to push his luck.

After kissing her lightly on the cheek he headed back to the lake for a last stroll. He must note his horoscope for this day, he thought -- clearly he was under a good sign.

CHAPTER SIX

After completing the remainder of the week's calls in Zurich, Matt was back in his New York apartment Saturday afternoon. Matt wanted to share the good news and the evening with Whitey, but locating him was always half the problem. Noting that there was a hot breeze blowing down Second Avenue, Matt decided to take a chance that Whitey was on his sailboat. He called for his car from the garage and drove out to Whitey's yacht club on Long Island.

Whitey was just tacking the 35' Peterson into the slip as Matt approached.

"Hey, Matt. Didn't expect to see you till tomorrow. Did you come in earlier? We could have gone for a sail."

"Just arrived. Wanted to bring you up to date. Terrific trip. I think I got the LeFevre account."

Whitey tightened the painter around the slip's cleat. He began to methodically fold the mainsail. Matt went on board to help.

"Well, I'm glad to hear that," Whitey said with the enthusiasm of someone who's heard 'that' several times before.

"Let me tell you. LeFevre & Cie is one of the most

sophisticated banks in Switzerland. They're running a lot of money and we've got a good shot at being a prime broker for them."

"Then they've come to the right place," responded Whitey as automatically as he furled the sail. Matt was getting far less attention than the sail's battens.

"Listen. Listen. This is going to be a great account."

Whitey turned to Matt -- his look said, "I'll believe it when the orders roll in." Out loud he said, "Great. Want to join us for dinner. Ann should be here any minute."

Matt gave up. Besides Whitey was right. What use are promises unless they translate into reality.

Dinner with Whitey and Ann only more sharply etched in Matt's memory his dinner with Christine in Geneva. The food at the restaurant had been prepared earlier that day and tasted it. In addition, Ann was Christine's opposite. Outspoken and demanding, Ann dominated the conversation with complaints and taunts. She had not joined Whitey on the sail because "it was difficult to get a tan on something that was always changing its angle." Matt knew that Whitey's interest in her was mostly physical -- dark and stately, Ann was decidedly attractive -- but it disturbed Matt anyway that Whitey could not find someone with more endearing qualities.

Matt spent the rest of the weekend in an anticlimactic state. Had he built everything up in his mind -- or did the future really hold possibilities?

Monday brought the usual routine at the office. The summer rally had not yet materialized and the ticker was edging downward. No one wanted to get caught in a sharp decline, so traders were staying clear of holding big positions. There were occasional pops in the Dow Jones -- either because of a vague opinion about the future of interest rates, or another takeover candidate surfaced -- but the broadly based averages were in a holding pattern.

Matt's business reflected the general malaise. Orders filtered in daily -- mostly in 5,000 and 10,000 share lots -- adequate to pay the overhead, but not enough to make any real money. The staff was even edgier than before Matt's trip -- the slowness of the days gave them ample time to worry. Matt attended to the routine without much enthusiasm. A slow market had that effect.

Thursday morning, after the 10 AM opening bell, the telex began to click. Jerry Stern checked the incoming message.

"Hey, Matt. I think it's for you."

"I'm only interested if it's an order."

"It may be. It's from your new friend, LeFevre."

Matt jumped up. The machine churned out the message.

"This is LeFevre & Cie. Geneva, Switzerland. July 29. Please buy 100,000 repeat 100,000 shares USOCO at the market carefully. Payment our account Morgan Guaranty. Request shares be held in nominee name, your choice. Recap all purchases at market closing to this telex number. Signed, Andre LeFevre."

"Allll rrright. You got it!" said Matt, as he slapped the side of the telex machine.

Matt excitedly called Whitey on the floor. Whitey's clerk, Terry, answered. Terry was given to a fair amount of elbow bending in the evening, and on slow days he usually disappeared between two and three in the afternoon, presumably to down a few. But he was fast and accurate while on the job -- the only important qualities for a floor clerk.

Normally, Matt would pass the order to Terry. This time he said, "Get Whitey. I got something to tell him."

Two minutes later Whitey came on. "What's up."

"Take an order. Buy 100,000 USOCO, market, carefully."

"I don't believe it -- who for?"

"Our new man in Geneva -- LeFevre and C.I.E." Matt spelled out the last abbreviation for emphasis.

"Way to go! A bottle of champagne on me tonight! Matt, I didn't think you could, but you've made a believer out of me now."

CHAPTER SEVEN

Whitey wrote down the order from Matt on a small pad, tore off the paper, folded it, and stuck it back in his order pad under the other pages. He did that because he didn't want other floor brokers, or the specialist in USOCO, to see the size of the order as he walked out to the trading post. That post, which in reality was a large oval booth containing several desks and clerical people, was the only place in the world where there was always a market for USOCO shares. As he approached the post, he glanced up at the video monitor which hung above it to check the last sale price of the stock. It read 32 3/4.

Jack McGrory was the market maker for USOCO. He was the senior partner of McGrory and Co., members New York Stock Exchange. He was second generation -- his father, William S., had founded the firm in the early 30's. Jack was now 65, rotund, jowly, and with a permanent set of knitted eyebrows, as if they were his main weapon to fight off impending retirement. One shoulder was perennially lower than the other as a result of forty years of leaning with one elbow on the post's trading counter.

As a market maker, Jack was responsible, according to the rules of the Stock Exchange, for making a "fair and orderly market" in USOCO stock. He did this with great skill -- and his trading abilities were amply reflected in his profit and loss statement.

The action today in USOCO had been rather slow. USOCO normally traded about 800,000 shares a day, making it a very liquid stock. But today there was little interest. Jack liked the stock -- at the moment he was long about 60,000 shares. He hoped that he could sell them up 1/4 point today -- that would yield him an easy 15 grand, not untypical of a day's pull.

Whitey looked down from the video screen and said to Jack, "How's USOCO?" This was floor talk for "What is the best bid and lowest offer for USOCO shares."

Jack snapped back, "32 1/2 - 3/4 -- 25,000 either way." Jack meant that the best bid to buy the stock was 32 1/2, and the lowest offer to sell the stock was 32 3/4. The amount bid and offered was 25,000 shares or any part thereof. The bid or the offer could have come from a brokerage house representing clients holdings, or from Jack's own trading position.

"What do you got to do?" asked Jack.

"3/4's, 25,000," said Whitey.

"Sold," said Jack.

Whitey had just bought 25,000 shares of USOCO at 32 3/4. He still had 75,000 shares left to buy -- but he was in no hurry. If he had bid for the whole 100,000 in one shot, Jack would only have been obligated to sell him the 25,000 he was offering at 3/4's. Jack would then have the upper hand in this negotiation game, if he knew the full extent of Whitey's buy interest. Whitey would risk running the price of the stock up.

After Jack and Whitey exchanged 'give-ups', meaning

their respective clearing firms, the transaction was complete. Your word was your bond on the floor of the New York Stock Exchange.

"How are you quoting it now?" asked Whitey.

"32 3/4 bid, offered at 33 -- 10,000."

'I'll take 10,000 at 3," said Whitey.

"Sold."

Whitey now had 65,000 shares left to buy. He sent a 'squad', a Stock Exchange messenger, with the report for the first 35,000 shares back to his booth. Terry then gave the reports up to Matt in the office by direct phone wire.

"32 3/4 bid for 20,000," said Whitey.

"Bid with you, 10,000 at 3," replied Jack. This meant Jack was a buyer along with Whitey, at the same time that he would be happy to sell stock to him.

It had been a slow day, but the other brokers gathered around the USOCO post noticed what was going on. Both the Merrill Lynch and Paine Webber brokers who were sellers in USOCO responded with offers. "I'll offer 20,000 at 33 said the Merrill broker. "10,000 at 3," said the Paine Webber broker.

"3 bid for 65,000," said Whitey.

"I sold you 20,000," said the Merrill man.

"I sold you 10,000," said Paine Webber.

"I sold you 35,000," said Jack, selling out the rest of his long position, and going short 10,000 on his sale to Whitey.

Whitey walked away.

"How's USOCO," said the Merrill broker.

"32 3/4 bid, offered at 33 1/4. 10,000 either way." Jack hoped to buy back the10,000 shares sold short to Whitey at 1/4 point less than the price Whitey had paid.

Back at his booth, Whitey called Matt on the phone. "Your order is complete at 33. To recap, you bought 25,000 at 32 3/4, and 75,000 at 33."

"Good job, Whitey." Matt was pleased -- the order had been executed within 1/4 of a dollar of the last sale. He quickly confirmed the purchase by telex to Raoul, who responded back, "Thank you very much. The commission is 4 cents per share."

That's 4 cents times 100,000, thought Matt, a four thousand dollar bill. Matt instinctively leaned back in his chair, smiled and said to no one in particular, "Now, that's what I call an order."

CHAPTER EIGHT

November 1985

The United States Oil Company is housed in an imposing glass and aluminum building off of I-45 near the NASA space center in Houston. The company's original name was Widdler Exploration and Drilling, founded back in 1901 right after Spindletop became a legend, by Darryl Widdler, an East Texan who had bought up cheap leases by the dozens till his money hit money and his luck hit rock bottom. He retained half the company, sold the other half to Lubbock Rigging, and used the proceeds of the sale to purchase more leases under his own name.

It wasn't genius that inspired Widdler to buy those leases -- Widdler knew little about oil. But he was a compulsive gambler -- he even would bet with any taker on which raindrop would hit the bottom of a windshield first. If Las Vegas had been a reality then, he would have been buying $5 chips instead of pieces of paper generated by geologists -- reports he could barely read, much less understand.

Eventually, the gamble paid off -- some of the leases Widdler held were in the right place and time. Widdler was smart enough not to sell the rights on his personally held leases immediately -- rather he held off until 1938 when he had run through the remainder of his cash. The good ones were bought by the Widdler-Lubbock Company; the remainder were dropped in the market. Widdler died not long after that, childless and penniless.

Widdler was barely active in the daily management of the company -- his love was gambling, not bureaucracy. Professional managers had been brought in -- the 30's Depression had provided the labor market with all the talent you wanted, and they no longer objected to the brutal East Texas climate and the still undeveloped social culture. Unfortunately, they too were limited in the knowledge of the oil industry. They were able to produce and sell rigging equipment effectively -- production and marketing were the basic subjects in business school -- but they were worse than novices at the oil lease and production end.

Trying to outsmart the locals, they had bought prospects which had encouraging geologists' reports, with the idea that they would be able to keep the big wells and lease off the other properties once another major oil pool was uncovered. They missed the mark entirely. The wells were low producers and the local companies didn't even bid on Widdler - Lubbock's offers to lease, mostly to spite the company that refused to syndicate the properties in the first place. By 1937, Widdler-Lubbock was close to the end of its resources.

The managers changed the name of the company to United States Oil and Rigging Company to make it sound more important and offered shares in the company to the public. They sold at $10 a share, par value, and the managment was relieved when they were able to push 1,000,000 of them out to buyers. They redoubled their efforts in rigging equipment and started to bring the company back to a reasonably sound state. During the war they produced floating bridges and pontoons, but returned to rigs when it ended. Occasionally an oversea's order would come in, to which USO&R paid special attention. The managers, having come from the North, were not as parochial as many of their Texas counterpart, and eagerly sought foreign

45

markets to strengthen its marketing base.

Eventually, USO&R set up foreign based representatives in Venezuela, Kuwait and Indonesia. Payments were often made by the smaller drillers in terms of local currencies and occasionally in exchange for prospects. The company, to use up its local currencies, often purchased additional properties or leases adjacent to the ones they already had. By the late 1940's, they were actively drilling in those locales; by the late 50's they were major refiners; and by the late 60's they had been paid huge sums in repatriation funds for the properties nationalized by the governments.

In addition to this activity, USO&R had developed an efficient pressure pump, which made the low production wells considerably more valuable. When the price of oil rose from $1 to $12, it began providing them with substantial returns on the formerly worthless property. With the excess funds being accumulated in the company, they began an active merger program, buying out many of the Texas companies that had laughed at their earlier drilling failures. The early 70's, with the huge increase in the price of oil, brought even greater wealth to the company. In 1975 they changed their name to United States Oil Company, added the logo USOCO to their letterhead, and shared their billing as the largest U.S. oil company only with Exxon and Mobil.

Herbert Kramer, USOCO's President, sat at his large, but otherwise non-descript, mahogany desk. Unlike the exterior of the building, the office was unpretentious, almost ascetic, reflecting Kramer's own disinterest in style. He had come to Houston as the corporate lawyer after a brief tenure in a waspy New York law firm. Despite his brilliance, he did not have the connections necessary to make partner in those days, so when his associate period was up he accepted a job with the Houston company.

USOCO had recognized his intelligence and was willing to pay for it. The salary was excellent but the personal and

46

social benefits were almost nil. As a Jew in a not-yet cosmopolitan city, Kramer and his wife were limited socially in the early years to Saturday night bridge with a small circle of friends. His rise within the company did not improve his attitude towards his gentile associates, and he harbored a special dislike of any group with anti-semitic reputation, deserved or not, such as WASPs, Southerners and Blacks. Naturally, Arabs and Iranians were very high on his hate list.

In his hands he held a memorandum from Owen Perry, his special assistant and aide-de-camp. In it, Perry made reference to the progress of USOCO's quarterly stock repurchase program. Each year USOCO bought back on the open market millions of its own shares, both to use for employee stock option plans and also to enhance the value of its outstanding shares.

In the third quarter of 1985, just ended, the company had repurchased 25 million shares, leaving about 750 million still outstanding. At $30 a share, the company's market value was $22.5 billion. These facts were not terribly newsworthy to Kramer -- he glanced at the numbers in the practiced manner of executive report reading. But his attention was stirred when the memo referred to the stock's action over the last few months. With one eye still on the report, Kramer picked up the phone and dialled Perry's number.

"Owen, your report suggests that there's a lot more interest in the stock than usual."

"Yes sir, I noticed a lot of buying -- I think the institutions are coming in big."

"Which institutions. Most of the big players we know are already up to their limits with USOCO shares."

The point had never occured to Perry. "Ah, well, I could look into it a bit more, if you like, sir."

47

"Of course I like. Call me back when you've got something."

Perry called down to the company's corporate relations department, Jim Harris. "What is the most recent run of shareholders you have."

"We show a lot of shares that are being held in a nominee name -- 'Monblank & Co.'"

The name meant little to Perry, who had never been to Geneva, and didn't catch the pun. "How many shares are they holding?"

"About 900,000. Does that mean anything to you?"

"Eh, hm, no. Funny name. Who's the broker who handled the order?"

"Matthew Allyn & Co."

"Are they any good?"

"Beats the wee outta me. I thought you guys had all the inside tracks with the stock market boys."

"Yeah, I'll call up to New York. Someone's gotta know something there."

"Okay. I'll take a closer look at the transaction sheets. Maybe something will pop up there."

Perry put calls through to three people. The first one, Max Adler, returned his call right away.

"Hey, Owen. How are things down in sweat city." Max hated the Houston climate and never failed to point it out. Owen, who had been his classmate at Duke University, was a good ole boy from West Texas, where summer meant hot and dry. He hated the humidity even more.

"Swell -- or sweltering. I dunno. I'm in air conditioning all day."

"What's up? You guys want me to do a leveraged buy out for you? Take the company private?" Max was an expert in financial deal making -- a risk arbitrageur.

"Yeah, right." The idea of a leveraged buy out involving $20 plus billion dollars was well beyond the ability of any likely purchasers or even any group of purchasers. Still, it made for a good running joke.

"Max, I have another question. You're in on the Street's rumor mill. What do you hear about our stock?"

"Ah, nothing. Nothing at all. Why? What's up?"

"Nothing particular. Just seems to be more than usual interest. Earnings should be level for a while, so buying it for a price/earnings play doesn't make much sense."

"Well, if I hear anything, I'll give you a call."

"Thank's anyway. See ya."

The next caller returned the call at 4:30 New York time, after the close of the market. Owen took a slightly different approach -- he didn't really trust the USOCO specialist.

"Jack, what's new down on the floor there? How's our stock going? I like to keep apace of how our stock's specialist is faring."

"Fine, fine. Hey, your company has been pretty active. I like that in a stock -- keeps me young."

49

Keeps you rich, thought Owen, who knew that specialists rarely lose when the stock is active. "Yeah, that volume's pretty high. Any rumors we're missing out on."

"Rumors? On your stock? Like what -- a takeover? That's about as likely as Russia going public." Jack laughed heartily at his own joke.

No progress here, thought Owen. "Anyone in particular doing the buying?"

"Jeez, I don't watch those kinds of things. I got a million floor brokers trading with me all day. Hey look, if I see a pattern, I'll give you a call."

Owen hung up and sighed. Maybe it was really nothing.

The last call came in at 7:00 Central Time just as Owen was leaving the office for the evening. It was from Jon Smathers, of Hillman, Flax, the company's investment bank. Smathers was always returning his calls in the evening, as if to prove that he was working even later and harder in New York.

"Owen, sorry I couldn't get back to you sooner, but your message didn't say it was urgent."

"It isn't. Just doing a bit follow-up. We've noticed more than the usual action on our stock on the Exchange -- we're wondering if there are any rumors that have missed our ears."

"None that have gotten to mine. Should I do some scouting for you?"

"No, thanks, we're already doing that at this end. But we appreciate your offer."

"Well, we will certainly call you promptly if we hear

anything." The tone in Smather's voice was a cross between obsequious and pompous. In another life and another time, Smathers would have made a terrific butler.

"You do that. I won't keep you from your busy schedule."

"Yes, I do have few more things to attend to this evening."

Yeah, right, thought Owen, as he hung up. Well, three strikes and you're out.

CHAPTER NINE

Max Adler was already rifling through various papers on his desk before he had even hung up the phone after his discussion with Owen. His offer to report any news to Owen was tempered by his own insatiable need for information. Whatever was not directly useful to Max himself would be passed on -- otherwise it would stick with him.

Max knew Owen from Duke, but they were barely acquaintances during the school years. Max was from Detroit, son of a deli owner, an immigrant from Poland. Owen was on the football team, not first string, but certainly good enough to make the West Texas town newspaper on a weekly basis. Max was the team's manager -- Max was always on the money side of any club involvements. Max would have completely forgotten Owen had he not noticed in the alumni guide that Owen had taken a position in the treasurer's department at USOCO. He then made it a point to look up Owen on his next trip to Texas. Owen would probably not have bothered to respond to his offer for a drink, had Max not already received a fair degree of publicity as a financial whiz.

Max Adler and Company actively followed and traded hundreds of stocks -- the company had twenty technical analysts just reviewing charts and numbers. This supported Max's main line of business, risk arbitrage. The term was something of a contradiction -- arbitrage, the buying and selling of goods in two markets simultaneously to benefit from the price differentials, was by definition riskless. Adding risk was a recent variation, an especially successful investment technique during the turbulent takeover period.

Max hoarded information the way some people hoard string. Owen had unwittingly provided him an additional length. Max's people had noticed that the stock showed unusual activity, but nothing quite specific enough from which to draw a conclusion. Max now knew that USOCO had found it unusual as well -- meaning that something must be going on.

Max carefully reviewed the numbers. Since July average daily trading volume was up approximately 100,000 shares per day, a meager amount considering USOCO's 750 million outstanding shares, but significant if they could all be attributed to one customer. Max did a ballpark calculation. If that purchaser had gone into the market every day from mid-July to mid November, that would be 100 business days worth of transactions, meaning that there could have been an accumulation of 10 million shares. A 1.3% ownership. At a cost of $300 million dollars. Who has that kind of money, he wondered.

Max knew that after an investor acculumates 5% of a particular stock, he must reveal himself to the SEC, the Securities and Exchange Commission. Another rough calculation -- 5% would cost over a billion dollars -- $1,125,000,000 to be exact. Big bucks. Very big bucks.

Who would want to take over USOCO? Max considered the possibilities.

The first possibility would be another larger company.

Given USOCO's size, that did not leave many -- just the other oil companies. But Exxon and Mobil wouldn't touch it because of probable antitrust action. Maybe Royal Dutch Shell, the Anglo-Dutch conglomerate. They already bought the remaining outstanding shares of Shell Oil, obstensibly because of excess cash in their corporate coffers. Max put a question mark after their name.

The second was a syndicate of traders. They would buy the stock, and hope to run up the price, and then sell out their position. It was risky at best -- the market or the stock could turn against the syndicate for any number of reasons. Besides, why choose USOCO when cheaper, and more interesting stocks, were available for this game.

The third was a foreign buyer -- not necessarily an oil company. Perhaps some company that wishes to have control of a large American business, or of a basic producer of a vital product. Certainly, none of the Comecon countries, or even Russia. It was unlikely that they had the cash to throw around. Max wondered. An Arab perhaps?

Suddenly another thought struck Max. Was this accumulation done for the benefit of "greenmail"? The buyer would purchase enough shares so that a prospective tender offer for the remainder would seem like a clear possibility. However, if the corporation's management decided to prevent even the possibility of the takeover, it would pay off the pursuer, who would handsomely profit on his accumulated stock position.

Max opened his drawer and pulled out a list of about 50 names and telephone numbers. The list was kept secluded, away from the eyes of even staff members. Most of the telephone numbers were unlisted, many to private lines.

Max made a series of telephone calls.

"Listen," he said to each name on the list. "I have something in mind." Everyone listened carefully. Max's plans were always worth their interest.

CHAPTER TEN

Jack McGrory sat in the den of his Park Avenue apartment watching the Islander's game on cable television. He was barely concentrating. In his mind he was recounting the action on the floor, something he hadn't done in years. He had been on the floor for so long that he rarely retained the day's activity much past the closing bell at 4 PM; so automatic were his actions.

But the recent activity in USOCO's stock caught his attention. He saw Whitey come to the post nearly every day -- not always to him directly, sometimes to the other junior partners -- but every day nonetheless. He knew Whitey to be a shrewd broker. You could rarely tell if he were about to buy or sell, picking up his shares in bits and pieces -- "working the order" as they say on the floor.

But something wasn't right. Whitey was at his post too often. He would expect to see the Merrill broker daily, or the one from Prudential Bache, but not the one from Matthew Allyn & Co. Of course, Whitey could have been doing $2 business, the floor term for doing the excess that other brokers couldn't or didn't want to handle themselves. (These brokers used to get paid $2 for every 100 shares they executed, hence the name.) He would have his clerk check Whitey's 'give-ups' tomorrow to see which brokerage houses were behind those transactions.

Jack shifted uneasily in his leather wing chair. It was his job to buy stock when people were selling and to sell stock when people were buying. If there was a big buying spree in USOCO stock, he would be forced to sell stock he did not own, which he would have to buy back at higher prices to cover the resulting short position.

The thought shook Jack. He went over to the bar and served himself two generous fingers of Irish. A picture of his daughter being showered with rice as she left St. Patrick's Cathedral looked down on him. Another of her sitting astride a horse in Southampton. The floor of the Stock Exchange had earned the McGrory family more than money, it bought respect. Before that they were Irish potato slingers -- the family's highest achiever having been a sergeant in the Brooklyn Police Department.

But in the 20's the Irish were allowed on the floor as clerks. They soon discovered that money was not fussy about who owned it. As other specialist firms dropped out of existance after the debacle in '29, William S. McGrory started his own. Being the newcomer, he was given the unknown names to deal with, such as United States Oil and Rigging -- it was a combination of doggedness, an innate ability to trade and a lot of luck that paid off in the end.

Although it was often said that if God were to come back to earth, He would come back as a specialist, losses were not unheard of. And when they occured, they had occasionally brought the firm down with them. Jack saw the chink in his armour. If investors got wind of a major buyer in the market, they would besiege the stock. Jack decided to do his damnedest to maintain a long position in USOCO.

But that too was risky. What if no rumor materialized? What if there were no big buyers out there? What if the market went down, and he was long a big chunk of stock? Jack poured another two fingers.

Jack's wife walked into the room, picked up a magazine and made herself comfortable in her personal chair. Jack hadn't really noticed her for the last ten years, but tonight she was especially invisible to him. When she casually said "How's the game going?" he nearly jumped out of his skin.

CHAPTER ELEVEN

Jonathan Smathers hung up the phone with Owen and turned slowly in his chair. It was true that he hadn't heard any rumors, but Nick Bianco, the firm's block trader, was plugged into the other major trading desks on the Street. He should know. Smathers decided to have a chat with him.

The trading desk closed at five, and traders were not the type to hang around their offices just to gather up brownie points. Smathers knew where Nick was likely to be at this hour. He threw on his overcoat and headed towards Harry's Hanover Square. The Wall Street area is as dead as any downtown financial district at night, except for a few oases, all bars, where brokers, traders and other pressured financial types came to unwind and swap stories. The bar area was four deep with regulars. In a far corner sat Nick, who seemed to be simultaneously talking and thinking. Good traders were like that -- dealing with things as if they had two brains handling disparate actions at the same time.

"Hello, Jon. How are you?" Nick said without much enthusiam. To Nick, Jon Smathers represented the ultimate banker WASP -- pin stripe suit, white shirt, club tie, tortoise shell glasses, fair skin. That was tolerable enough, but Smathers had always overacted the role, at least, that's how it seemed to Nick. But then, Nick, short, dark, bearded, had

59

always had a special dislike for the fair haired set.

"Hi there, Nick. Long time no see. Am I disturbing you?"

Nick picked up on the cue. "No. Not at all. Care to join us for a drink?"

"Of course. Thanks. I'll buy you one." Nick immediately knew that the meeting in Harry's was not accidental. Smathers, a yuppie investment banker type, did not "hang out" with the traders, and certainly would never offer to pay.

"What's up," asked Nick, now wanting to get to the point.

"Oh, nothing particular. Thought I'd get some fresh air and a quick one before I went back to work."

Smather's transparent words put Nick even more on guard. "Yeah sure."

"Let's sit someplace more quiet."

"Right." Nick was starting to get annoyed with all this roundabout chatter.

The two moved to a cocktail table towards the back. Nick stared into the crowd. He would wait for Smathers to make the move.

"You know, I just got a call from someone down at USOCO. They were wondering if there were any rumors on the stock."

All this for rumors on a stock? Nick knew there had to be some kicker to this. After all, the firm had strict rules as to a "Chinese Wall" separating the information flow between the investment bankers and the traders in the company. Nick took the bait anyway -- his trading needed help -- legal or not.

"No. No rumors. Just the usual action of someone trying to make money in a dead market."

"But there is unusual action. Right?"

"Right."

"And a rumor in this market, combined with those big trading volume increases, would probably cause the stock to really pop. Right?"

What is this, thought Nick, amateur night at the stock exchange follies. "Right again."

"See, that's why USOCO is concerned. Their stock is very vulnerable right now. So, if you hear any rumors, you should call and tell me anything you hear so I can inform them right away."

"You got it." Nick didn't think the price of the drink was worth this conversation. Something else, something worth far more than $2.50, had to be going on, he decided.

"By the way, what is Hillman's position in the stock?"

Nick thought for a minute. Inadvertently or otherwise, Smathers was cluing him in that something was brewing with USOCO stock. He decided to respond despite the ethics. "No position. We're about flat. Why?"

"You'll inform me of any position changes, won't you? For internal purposes only -- I wouldn't tell USOCO, of course."

Then what the hell do you want to know for, wondered Nick. What does this "internal purposes" shit mean? "Yeah, sure. Anything you want."

"Good. Good. Well, I better get back to work. Thanks for your time." Smathers put some money down on the table.

"Gee, let's do it again, soon," Nick answered, but Smathers missed the veiled disdain completely.

Outside, Smathers stopped at the nearest telephone booth and put in a long distance call to Boston.

"Betsy. How are you? Listen, I'm at a phone booth, so I'll be quick. How much money do we have in that little money market account we have together? About 50 grand. Okay. Don't do anything with it -- I've got some new ideas. Terrific. That's my girl. Big kiss to you too. I'll call you later. Bye."

Smathers returned to the office to do some more work. Actually, most of the time was spent reading magazines -- something he could have done just as easily at home -- but it looked more impressive to be seen at the office until eleven.

CHAPTER TWELVE

Nick rolled Smathers' comments over in his mind as he drove his Jaguar down the FDR Drive the next morning. Smathers wasn't a trading type -- he had never displayed any interest in "buyin'em and sellin'em". For him to get involved in the discussions on trading positions, there had to be a good reason. No smoke without fire.

The management at USOCO was nervous about something. Otherwise they wouldn't be bothered about the volume increases. A possible accumulation by an investor? A takeover? That would be worrisome to the big boys at USOCO.

Nick was the senior equity trader at Hillman, Flax. He had gotten there the hard way. At 40, he already had 22 years experience under his belt. He started as a squad on the floor, maneuvered his way into a clerk's position at a small OTC trading firm, eventually becoming a market maker at a major firm. Hillman, Flax wooed him away with a salary that he would have described as "obscene" had he not been earning it himself.

He was talented, politically savvy, and just plain street smart from his Brooklyn days. Without any formal education, he was a student of psychology. He knew how fear and greed affected people, emotions that were magnified to the worst degree in investors. His ability to trade with perfect emotional detachment had been his key to survival.

Even so, Nick was under great pressure to perform. The trading desk was a profit center and the past year had been tough. Flat to down markets make it difficult to generate trading profits, especially at the level that the firm expected. Nick was the partner in charge -- but that didn't make it a lifetime sinecure -- two years of below average results could land you on the street. Truth to tell, Nick needed a big hit in the market.

When Nick got to the office, he instructed Joanne, his trading assistant, to indicate buy interest for the firm on the AUTEX, the computer block trading system. By noontime, he had purchased 300,000 shares of USOCO in two blocks of 150,000 shares each.

At first, he was going to forget about Smathers request for information, but his innate psychological instinct dictated otherwise. He reached for the phone.

"Jonny." Nick deliberately used a nickname that he presumed Smathers loathed. "It's Nick. Just called to tell you that we like USOCO here. We're gonna trade around a core position of a half million to a million shares."

"Really? Thanks, Nick. I appreciate your call."

Nick hoped that he was going to be right on USOCO -- he couldn't afford to be wrong. The expenses of supporting a wife and three kids in Englewood Cliffs were bad enough, and to that he had to add the cost of keeping a mistress on West 73rd Street.

CHAPTER THIRTEEN

As Matt unlocked the door to the office, he could hear the telex machine humming. Right on cue, thought Matt, as he put his winter health food breakfast -- a hard roll with cream cheese and hot coffee -- down on his desk. He checked the machine; it said, as it had virtually every day for the last four months, to buy 100,000 shares of USOCO for the account of LeFevre & Cie., signed Andre LeFevre.

LeFevre used Matthew Allyn & Co for this transaction only. Despite Matt's suggestion to Raoul during their infrequent telephone calls to expand the business, LeFevre stuck to only the purchases of the USOCO stock. Not that Matt had any complaints. Every transaction went smoothly; funds were always available on the delivery date at Morgan Guaranty. It meant a daily $4,000 commission payment to Matt's firm -- a goddam golden goose.

Of course, it did require some skill on the firm's part. By trading in bits and pieces throughout the day, sometimes selling and buying back to confuse the other brokers, Whitey managed to start a major accumulation in the stock without alerting the rest of the market. LeFevre was also smart to use Matthew Allyn & Co.-- the firm's size relative to the big boys made the other brokers less suspicious of any major activity.

Whitey came in soon after and started munching on his own breakfast -- nova scotia on a bagel with a bermuda onion and a Coke.

"Good morning, m'boy." Whitey seemed unusually cheery.

"Morning. You must have had a good night's, uh, sleep."

Whitey chuckled. 'You've got to hear about this one." A friend of Whitey's in the garment business had given Whitey the names of two sisters, reputed to be fantastic. "Well, I called them up, Pam and Barb are their names -- they're identical twins. They bill themselves out as a "twin-cestuous experience." Whitey then went on to recount all the details of his three hour, four hundred dollar episode, laughing at his previous night's travail.

Jerry came into the office on the tail end of the story, so Whitey retold the whole event all over again. Each telling produced slightly more deviation, slightly more sex. Everyone roared -- Whitey laughed harder each time he repeated it, reliving his own experiences vicariously.

At 9:30, Whitey left to go to his station on the floor -- to do his "constitutional", as he referred to the daily trek to the USOCO post. Matt stayed "upstairs" to handle the other normal business. Spirits were definitely up at the firm. The morning's sarcastic repartee was slowly being replaced by more convivial good humor. The sales assistants lingered longer in the evening to clean up their work; fewer errors passed through the trading accounts. The rest of Wall Street's firm were still waiting in November for the summer rally -- but at Matthew Allyn & Co. the bull market was already there.

Matt's personal routine had changed only slightly as a

result of the bonanza -- cabs downtown instead of the IRT, bigger tips for the shoeshine men, and veal chops milanese instead of pasta at Fiorella's. The rest went into the firm's capital account. The bear market that was engulfing Wall Street was a constant reminder to Matt that hard times were only a few trades away. Bear markets had a way of weeding out the self styled bull market geniuses -- traders who thought that they were brilliant simply because they were in the right place, betting on the right thing during a priod of rising prices.

Matt's phone rang.

"Allo, Matt. This is Christine Evins. You remember, from LeFevre & Cie." The last part was completely unnecessary, Matt remembered very well.

"Christine. It's great to hear from you," Matt boomed, causing every one on the trading desk to turn around.

"Well, I called to tell you that I am coming to New York."

"Terrific," said Matt, with considerable natural enthusiasm. "When?"

"Wednesday evening. I'll be staying at the Mayfair Regent." The Mayfair was a favorite among Europeans and foreign diplomats. Pretty nice digs on a secretarial salary.

"You're here on business, then?" Matt guessed. "Are you coming alone?"

"Yes. Yes to both questions."

"Well, then I'll pick you up at the airport."

"That's not necessary. I can make my way." Christine

clearly did not want to be rushed. "But I'll give you a call when I arrive."

"I'll be waiting." Matt gave Christine his home number. He was glad she gave him very short notice -- patience was not one of Matt's greatest virtues.

Wednesday morning Matt noticed something that would not have concerned him otherwise. The usual daily telex was signed by Raoul Hengler, not Andre LeFevre. That must mean that both Christine and Andre were away from the office at the same time. Matt wondered if they were also both at the Mayfair.

CHAPTER FOURTEEN

Matt waited for Christine in the lobby of the Mayfair. The lounge was designed to recreate an elaborate sitting room atmosphere; immense floral pieces filled with gladiolas and forsythia upstaged the huge Austrian glass chandelier in the room's center. The effect was formal and feminine, the perfect atmosphere, thought Matt, for a nascent relationship.

Christine emerged from the elevator wearing a cerise silk dress. Matt, whose knowledge of flowers did not go past long stem roses, found himself comparing the striking reds and yellows of the flowers to her dress and hair. Matt was astounded by his own awareness. His sensual perceptions seemed to becoming more acute.

To his own surprise, Matt greeted her formally. Was it the room that generated that stiffness in him, or the fear that Andre LeFevre was just around the corner, about to walk into the room any minute?

"I love this room," she said, indicating that this was not her first visit to the hotel.

"Oh, you've stayed here before?" asked Matt.

"Oh, about once a year," she replied, looking vaguely

around the room.

"But, you're here on business."

Christine didn't answer. "I'll have a kir," she said instead. Matt ordered the same for both of them. He noticed that the relaxed feeling that ended their previous meeting was not present today.

"I noticed that Andre LeFevre is also out of town."

Christine's face hardened. "But, how did you know that?"

"Well, I can put two and two together. He is here, isn't he? He came to New York as well." Matt almost added "with you" but thought the better of it.

Christine looked at him for a minute and then started laughing. "Is that what you think? Is that why you have been so formal?"

"I give up," said Matt, flustered by his faux-pas, "what did I say?"

"It's not you. It's this whole, eh, thing. No, Andre LeFevre is not here, he's in Monte Carlo. But that's important. Because if he weren't there, I wouldn't be here."

Matt was lost. "You will tell me what's going on," he said plaintively.

"I guess I'll have to -- since you have already figured out so much."

"Uh, yes?" Matt drew a breath as one expecting to hear bad news.

"Well. You see. Andre LeFevre likes to go to Monte Carlo every year for vacation. But not with his wife. With his mistress."

Matt was catching on. "But he tells his wife he is going to New York."

"Yes, that way she doesn't expect him to return for the weekend. So he sends me instead of himself, so there is 'proof' of someone being here. I register in the hotel under the name LeFevre so there is a bill in that name. Also, if a call comes through, I instruct the switchboard to only take a message. Then I call Mr. LeFevre in Monaco to tell him to contact his wife. Also, I buy her a gift at one of the New York stores, like Tiffany or Bergdorf Goodman's, which I leave in the check room of the airport in Geneva. Mr. LeFevre picks it up on his return from Monaco, so that he has it in his luggage when he returns home. It has worked very well."

Matt blew out a long breath. "And you get a vacation in New York in the best hotel."

"Yes, and anything I want at Bergdorf's. Do you like my dress? It's from last year's excursion."

"Yes," he said, pleased that he had already noticed it. "I like it very much. Very much." The sense of relief was so acute that he was almost babbling.

Christine let out a girlish giggle. Everything was relaxed again.

"Let's switch to champagne," he said. "I want to make a toast. To Andre, of course."

Matt took Christine to dinner at Fiorella's, an Italian restaurant on the East Side in walking distance of the hotel. The restaurant is divided into three parts, an enclosed outdoor cafe, a bistro, and a formal restaurant. In keeping with the evening's cachet, Matt chose the formal section. Matt noticed that Christine studied the menu carefully, and picked the chicken triestino, one of the less expensive items. She did not pick the house speciality the last time either -- a serious concern for Matt's wallet? To compensate, Matt asked for a double order of the caviar appetizer for both of them.

"I would really like to see your office," she said, towards the end of the meal.

"My office?" Matt was making a mental comparison to that of LeFevre's -- a visit to the office was guaranteed to deflate any bubble of glamour he had managed to create.

"Yes, you mentioned it last time, when we had dinner in Geneva."

Matt had forgotten. "Well, I would love to have you, but it's always such confusion. I couldn't promise you a good time."

Christine looked disappointed. "I understand. I'd be in your way. That's how they are at LeFevre. No one wants to show me around the trading room because I'm a bother to them. Besides, because I'm a woman, they think I wouldn't understand what's going on anyway."

Matt knew what she was getting at. Even in New York, which is fairly open to women in the financial houses, the Stock Exchange was still a male bastion.

"I have a better idea," said Matt. "I'll have Whitey show you around the floor of the Exchange. Now that is really interesting -- much more so than a bunch of people staring at video screens and shouting into phones."

"I'd love it. When?"

"How about Friday? Then, while you're still dizzy from the floor, we'll have lunch at the Exchange."

"Wonderful. That really sounds like fun. And I'll make a report and give it to Mr. LeFevre. Maybe then he'll start doing business with you," she said, with mock authority.

"But LeFevre already does business with us. Every day."

Christine knitted her brow. "That's odd, when I asked the clerk in the back office for your telephone number, they said they never heard of you. I had to use international information to get it."

"You should have asked Raoul Hengler for our number. He certainly has it." Matt laughed at his understatement.

Christine shrugged. She considered telling him that all the brokers used by the firm have their name in the central registry. But instead she said, "What time shall I meet you on Friday?"

After dinner, Matt walked Christine back to the hotel, only three blocks away. Matt debated whether he should pressure her a bit more this time. He wanted to see her again during her stay -- he didn't want to put her off right away. But the after dinner Cointreau had heightened his slightly submerged passion. Matt was trying to work out the right approach while keeping up the small talk. Hotels were especially hard to handle, there usually was no reason not to part in the lobby.

By the time they reached the entrance, Matt had decided to ask to accompany her to her door, and then suggest another night cap. Just as he was about to make his offer, she turned and said, "Would you care to see my suite of rooms. Andre LeFevre always arranges for the best, and they are really quite magnificent."

"Delighted," he said, unhesitatingly. Was she just teasing him, he wondered.

The suite was indeed lovely -- it was furnished in regency style, and both the sitting room and the bedroom had fireplaces as central focal points. Matt pretended to look at all the artwork, even though it was of more standard hotel quality, undoubtedly to dissuade thieves. Matt looked especially closely at the one over the couch, and when Christine knelt on the couch to see what attracted his attention, Matt turned, held her, and when she did not resist, kissed her. They slid down somewhat awkwardly onto the couch together while still in the embrace, Matt sensing that she was enjoying each caress of their lips and tongue as much as he.

"So you are really not interested in art at all," she said mockingly.

"*Au contraire.* But in this case I prefer the live artwork to the painted."

"Do you also prefer being so uncomfortable?"

Matt pulled her up and led her into the bedroom. While she waited, he took off his shirt and trousers. Then he gently unzipped her dress and laid it on the boudoir chair. Underneath she was wearing a silk camisole and slip. Still standing, he pressed his body against hers and pulled the camisole over her head. There was no bra underneath -- her full round breasts needed none. He then reached down to

74

pull off her slip and panty hose. As he knelt to bring the clothes to her feet, an incredibly intense surge of sensation went through him as he became overwhelmed by the beauty of her body. He pressed his head into her belly and she reached down to pull him up and to her. They kissed passionately in a standing position until they slowly became aware of their discomfort and moved, without unlocking their embrace, onto the bed.

The next day, Matt sent two dozen red and yellow gladiolas to her room.

CHAPTER FIFTEEN

From the glassed-in visitor's gallery located on the mezzanine of the New York Stock Exchange, people can see brokers and traders moving below them in furious ant-like non-stop activity. A continuous din rises -- not quite the shouting matches that characterize the commodity exchange -- but still unnerving. A forty foot long electronic ticker tape, suspended about 20 feet above the trading floor, with symbols and numbers meaningless to the casual observer, adds to the distraction. Pieces of paper cover the floor like sawdust in the butcher store. For most uncomprehending tourists it is something to view in awe for fifteen minutes, and then to move on the the next attraction in the downtown area.

Actually being on the floor has a different quality. Men in undistinctive light blue cotton jackets are constantly jostling, or being jostled, by others mainly because bodies take less importance than the transaction at hand. Eyes are either directed at the suspended ticker, or at the video monitors attached to each trading post, unconsciously checking prices, trading volumes, and stock activity. Standing in the center is akin to being at the main gate of Grand Central Station at rush hour, but without the politeness. That is exactly how Christine felt.

Matt had arranged for Whitey to bring her to the floor on

Friday before lunch. A special pass is required and a visitor must be escorted by a floor member, a job which suited Whitey very well. Being on the floor with a tall honey blond was similar to being spotted at Southampton with a Rolls Royce -- your stock-in-trade was guaranteed to increase. And with volume off in anticipation of the weekend, there were plenty of floor personnel willing to shift their eyes from the ticker to Whitey.

"Hey, jumpball. H'yaaa." Floor brokers were not noted for their graciousness. Christine knew better than to ask for a translation. She had been in crowds of men before.

Whitey introduced her to the clerks, the other members of J Booth, where Whitey had his telephone lines, and to some of the floor governors, who monitored the activity. He eventually brought her around to Jack McGrory, who was used to entertaining visiting firemen, and who already had perfected his spiel on the importance of the role of the specialist in the preservation of capitalism and the American economy.

Jack showed Christine his 'book', which is where he writes in the different bid and offer prices waiting to be executed. Christine was astounded at the physical size of the book, she had expected something akin to a Victorian counting house ledger. Instead it was small enough to fit into the palm of his hand, and it was filled with numbers and notations in tiny script. Not that the contents were secret -- he showed her every page -- bids for the stock at lower price, offers for the stock at a higher price. From what Christine could see, there were as many bids on one side as on the other. Whitey had done a good job at keeping his bids secret.

Jack extended his presentation a few extra minutes with Christine -- most of the visitors are far less attractive. Besides he was charmed by her accent.

"You must be from France," he asked, in an absolutely guileless manner. It was years since Jack made any headway with the ladies.

"No, Geneva."

"Here on vacation?"

"No, business." Christine liked the sense of importance it connoted.

"Oh, who do you work for?"

"LeFevre et Compagnie. A Geneva bank. Do you know them?"

Jack didn't understand the pronunciation, and asked her to repeat it, then spell it. Jack was beginning to sense a connection. Here was Whitey entertaining a representative of a foreign bank, apparently in New York for the purpose of visiting Matthew Allyn and Co. Could they be the real buyers behind the USOCO purchases, he wondered. He put the notation of the firm's name in his pocket and made a mental note to have the company checked on.

CHAPTER SIXTEEN

Matt waited at the entrance to the Stock Exchange Luncheon Club on the seventh floor of the Exchange's building. He saw the express elevator on his left open and disgorge several brokers including Whitey and Christine. Jack McGrory, his curiosity peaked, had accompanied them up the elevator, but found out little more. Jack nodded to Matt, but waited at the entrance for his guest, while Matt and the other two walked passed the large statue of a bull and bear locked in mortal combat, the Exchange's symbol of Wall Street, into the dining area.

The luncheon club is a large, sparsely decorated room, whose most prominent feature is a massive clock against the far wall. It seems to serve as a reminder to the diners that time is money. Towards the front is the clambar, filled with iced barrels of oysters and clams from Long Island waters, and manned by one of the most proficient shuckers Matt had ever seen. The number of filled tables is inversely correlated to the level of activity on the trading floor -- the slower the day, the more the diners.

Only members of the Stock Exchange are entitled to eat at the Luncheon Club -- guests have to be accompanied by a member. The food is simple, even by some standards, mundane. But the aura of being a men's club and its exclusivity added to Chistine's excitement -- in Switzerland her access to such things was limited by her role of secretary.

Whitey and Matt reviewed with Christine what she had just seen on the floor because they knew how confusing the mechanics of trading appeared to outsiders. "Now, Christine, the whole system works because of two basic principles: fear and greed. People buy because their greed tells them the price of the stock will go higher, and they sell because they fear the stock will go to zero before they can get out. An oversimplification, maybe, but without it we wouldn't be doing any business."

Christine grinned. Many of the customers she met at LeFevre had expressed exactly those sentiments.

"Fear and greed know no national boundaries," she said. "However, we have discretion at LeFevre for our customer's investments, so most of them are not concerned where their funds are, as long as they are profitable at the end of the year."

"I sure hope that all the USOCO stock that we've bought for your customers over the last few months works out well for them," responded Whitey. "I think we've bought millions of shares."

"I'm not aware of any USOCO stock purchases," said Christine with surprise. "I told Matt earlier that I'm not even aware of your doing business with LeFevre & Cie."

Whitey laughed -- he dismissed her ignorance to general stupidity on the part of a secretary.

"Well, all the trades have been settled properly and been paid for by LeFevre, right, Matt? So I guess there's something going on at LeFevre that you just don't know about."

Whitey was being harsh, but Christine didn't care. There was something going on that she didn't know about, and that disturbed her. It also disturbed Matt -- he knew that Christine was well plugged in at LeFevre, and her lack of knowledge about the business was definitely strange.

Across the room, Jack McGrory sat with Max Adler, the risk arbitrageur. Jack and Max had been friends for years. In fact, Jack was one of Max's more important sources of capital for his arbitrage activities. Jack was a great specialist, but when it came to longer term investing he preferred to have Max handle his money.

Max had been eyeing Christine across the room -- she certainly added decor to the spartan dining room. Jack noticed Max's attention.

"Max, if we were only thirty years younger, eh."

'Do you know who she is, Jack?"

"As a matter of fact, she was just visiting me on the floor. Whitey Whitehill brought her over."

"Who's he with?"

"He's the floor partner from Matthew Allyn and Co." Jack seemed a little agitated when he mentioned that name. Neither Whitey's nor Matt's name meant anything to Max, but he made a quick mental notation in his computer-brain.

"And who's she, Jack. Just another bimbo."

"No. Not at all. She's a representative from a Swiss bank."

"Oh. Which one?"

Jack pulled out the piece of paper in his pocket. He showed it to Max.

"Well, well. It's LeFevre & Cie." said Max.

"Sounds like you know them?"

"Sure. They're one of the biggest private banks in Geneva. Big, important clients. Very well reputed."

Both men fell silent, as connections and relationships began to click in their minds.

CHAPTER SEVENTEEN

Matt usually gave less than ten minutes a day to the organization of his social life, but after lunch on Friday, he wasted nearly an hour in just choosing a restaurant to take Christine to that evening. After having rejected some of the better French (too overblown for the occasion), Italian (had Italian on Wednesday), and steakhouse (too heavy) restaurants, he settled on Chatfield's, comfortable but with a well thought out menu, and best of all, close to his apartment. He had even considered cooking at his own place, but decided that his limited culinary skills of thin steaks grilled on a miniscule terrace combined with some corny attempt at a romantic table setting were something that only a wide eyed country girl would appreciate. And Christine certainly was not that.

The choice proved to be perfect -- the restaurant's homey flavor had thoroughly relaxed Christine, and she displayed only the mildest of resistance when he suggested going back to his apartment. For a bachelor, he had done a pretty fair job of decorating -- he did not understand why some of his single friends put so little energy in a place where they spent so much time. He was especially proud of his art collection. He could not afford 'name' artists, but had bought very carefully at lesser shows and estate sales, where the talent far outstripped the price.

Christine made some gratifying comments about Matt's taste, and spent a few minutes admiring the paintings. There was one that particularly atttracted her, a French lithograph of a man in a cafe, which hung in a corner over his desk. As she stepped closer to look at it, her eye caught something lying on the desk of even far more interest.

"I see a copy of a telex from LeFevre. I recognize the answer back number."

Had Matt unconsciously left it there? "Yes, we told you we are active with them. Here, this is an order to buy 100,000 USOCO. We have been buying every day for months."

"I don't understand. I am familiar with many of the client's portfolios. Very few have any USOCO holdings at all."

"I think this is for some special customers. Andre had hinted very strongly of some new Middle Eastern connections."

"Arab connections? There are no Arab connections. Andre has a stong dislike for thc Middle East since he got badly hurt in the Kuwait Stock Exchange."

Matt knew what she was referring to. The Kuwaiti Exchange had been a high flyer for months until it burst, crashing far more severely than the New York Exchange in 1929, leaving behind a pile of financial carnage. So Andre was involved in that, Matt mused, surprised that such an astute banker could have been caught up in such a game.

"Then who is he buying the stock for?" asked Matt, knowing that the answer to that was really none of his business.

"I wonder who is sending this telex. Matt, I'm going to do some checking around when I return."

"Well, if there is a problem, I don't want to know. I like the four grand they send me daily."

"The four what."

"Oh, nothing." Matt suddenly felt mercenary. "Just an expression."

"By the way, Christine, does Andre know you are here? Seeing me that is?"

"No. I had no reason to mention it to him."

"Then, don't. Eh, you shouldn't mix business and pleasure." Matt didn't want to seem overly concerned -- the evening was beginning to become too heavy. Christine sat down in a corner chair, almost as if to brood.

Matt walked over to her, and without saying anything took her hand and slowly guided her into the bedroom. He unzipped the back of her dress and placed a kiss on the nape of her neck. He slowly moved down her spine, carefully pulling away clothing with each new kiss. By the time he reached her waist, he could have barely remembered how to spell Andre's last name.

CHAPTER EIGHTEEN

After his return from Monaco, Andre LeFevre held a brief meeting with Raoul in his office after the close of business. His "New York" trip had been successfully concluded -- either his wife didn't know, or knew, but preferred not to cut off the source of gifts, this time from Tiffany's, quite yet. In any case she had greeted him with true wifely ardor, so to his mind, all was well.

Raoul was recounting the events of the past week. "We continued to purchase our usual daily allotment, 100,000 shares, so that now our holdings are up to 11,000,000 shares exactly. However, I think the market is starting to get wind of things. The volume is increasing, over and above our dealing, and the price is inching up, even though the rest of the market is still quiet."

"How many more shares can we accumulate before we become obvious."

"Well, hopefully we can get to 30 million -- that would give us about a 4% holding -- enough to make an impact with the company, but less than the 5% necessary for full disclosure."

"Do you think that USOCO has any idea of what's going

on?"

"They must. Kramer is smart. He had to be to get where he is in that organization. I've been to America, and I know that Texas is not exactly a Jewish stronghold."

"What else to we know about Kramer?"

"Only what's in the American Who's Who. We should know more before we make our play."

"I agree. Let me call some friends in New York who might have had contact with him. We don't want to go into this too blindly."

After Raoul left, Andre picked up the private phone and direct dialed a New York telephone number.

"George, this is Andre LeFevre. How have you been?"

"*Bonjour,* Andre," replied George Hendricks, LeFevre account manager at Hillman Flax, in the most hideous accent. "Where are you? In New York?"

"No, in Geneva. It doesn't look like I'll be in New York for a while."

"Too bad. The boys here always enjoy our little chats with you," commented George, with the usual salesman's palaver.

"Well, your firm can be of help on a very simple matter."

"Ask away. Anything we can do."

"I know Hillman is very close to USOCO. Don't you handle all their offerings."

"Correct. A great customer."

"Well, one of our customers is going to visit with Herb Kramer at some private affair he is hosting in Texas. But, you see, he is an Arab, and doesn't know the first thing about Kramer, or Texas, for that matter, and would like to get some information. I'll fill him in on Texas but if you could help with Kramer, you know, the little things, so that he doesn't embarrass himself."

"Like Kramer being very religious. Ha!" said George. The thought of the Arab and the Jew meeting in Texas was funny.

"Yes, exactly. I knew I could rely on you."

"I'll get one of the juniors to work on it. When do you need it."

"Within a week would be fine. We are very grateful, as always."

"Our pleasure," which is business shorthand meaning: I hope you repay us with more business soon.

After finishing the conversation with Andre, George walked across the floor to Jon Smathers office.

"Jon, you're quite familiar with the USOCO account. Could you help me on a little matter. It's for one of our Swiss bank customers."

"Sure," said Smathers, who in fact hated to be asked to do 'little' projects.

George outlined the request.

"Why so much detail? Don't the Swiss know how to

handle themselves in Texas?"

"Well, it isn't for them -- it's for one of their Middle Eastern customers. Some big meeting in Texas that Kramer is hosting."

"Really." Things were starting to click in Smathers head. "I'll get someone on it right away."

"Much obliged as always."

"Uh, by the way, which Swiss bank did you say it was."

"I didn't," replied George, used to holding his counsel. "But it's LeFevre & Cie. Mean anything to you?"

"No, not at all. Just curious." After George left, Smathers made a careful notation of the name on his calendar pad.

CHAPTER NINETEEN

Owen Perry was just finishing his quarterly report on new stock ownership. In it he commented that a company named 'Monblank', obviously a nominee name, seemed to be accumulating a lot of shares, adequate to account for the rise in the trading volume, but that he had no insight into who the actual owners were. Further, the trading for that company was all handled through Matthew Allyn & Co., a small New York stockbroker. Owen concluded that there was little of importance to be derived from this -- particularly since Owen presumed that a serious investor would use a major brokerage house to handle the accumulation.

Owen's secretary indicated that Jon Smathers was on the line.

"Hello, Jon. Any news for me."

"Not really. I know that the activity in USOCO has created some interest on the part of our own block trader, nothing of any great magnitude, but I thought I would pass it on."

Owen knew that Hillman had taken a position two weeks ago. So why was Smathers only calling now?

Smathers continued. "I hear through the grapevine that some Arabs are coming to visit Kramer."

"Are you kidding? Arabs. With Kramer. He's got more Israeli bonds than Heinz has pickles. You must be plugged into the wrong grape."

"Oh, heavens, I must be." Smathers sounded especially ingratiating. "Sorry."

"Well, who cares. Look, I have a question for you. Have you ever heard of a company called 'Monblank'?"

"I've heard of a mountain by that name, but no company? Why?"

"Mountain?" Geography was not Owen's best topic. "Uh, no reason. Just something that popped up on the ownership run. Forget it."

"Of course. Well, got to get back to the salt mines here. I'll call if I hear anything else."

"Right. You do that."

As Smathers hung up the phone, a thought hit him. He went over to Polk's Directory of Banks and opened it to the alphabetical listing. He noted that LeFevre & Cie. was headquartered in Geneva, Switzerland, the same place as the mountain. Smathers slammed the book shut and absent mindedly returned to his desk. The ideas of Arabs visiting Kramer was nonsense. Then why the urgency to know all about him.

Smathers knew that there was something of significance in process -- but he could not mesh all the pieces. Fortunately, in the trading business, it doesn't matter if you know why you are right, as long as you are right.

Smathers phoned down to Nick Bianco on the trading desk.

"Nick, this is Jon Smathers. How's it going."

"Yeah, fine. What's up." The constant ringing of phones heard in the background was not an inducement to gracious conversation.

"Just checking up on the USOCO position. Want to keep them posted, you know."

Nick knew all right -- he knew that USOCO would know who held the stock from sources other than Smathers. What was Smathers' game, he wondered.

"Well, we have a core position of about 400,000 shares that we are trading around. Otherwise, nothing of interest. The price is up 1/4 from yesterday, at 35. It seems to be just starting to move up."

"Oh, how about the options on USOCO. Are they moving up too?"

"Haven't been watching them."

"Ah, could you check the August 50 calls -- just to get an idea."

"Yeah, sure," Nick mumbled. He was head of the trading desk, not a customer's representative at the Palm Beach office. Nick turned to the Quotron machine and plugged in some letters. "Looks like the're selling for $1. Not much action."

"Gee, thanks, you've been very helpful. I"m sure USOCO will appreciate it."

"Your wish is but my command," with such sarcarasm he could not see how Smathers could have missed the point. But Smathers had already taken the phone away from his ear. He hung up on Nick and went outside to a phone booth and put through a credit card call to Boston.

"Betsy, hi, honey. I've got to be brief, I'm calling from a phone booth. Have you got a pencil. I would like you to take down some options trades. Call Burman at Merrill and put in the orders in your name. Are you ready."

Smathers listed the trades he had wanted to make -- 300 contracts of the August 50 call options, selling for a $1 an option, or $100 per contract. In total, $30,000 worth of options. Since they were long term, out-of-the money call option contracts on USOCO, they were selling very cheaply. But when and if the price of USOCO approached $50 a share, then the value of the options could rise dramatically --perhaps twice, three or four times their value. Or more. It meant that if Smathers were right during the next nine months, he would make it big, very big, on very little down. But if he were wrong, he would lose it all. That was the essence of the options market.

"Oh, and Bets, be sure, I mean absolutely positive, not to mention my name. But if I'm right, I'll make lots of money. And part of that is yours, too. Call you later for a report."

Good old Bets, he thought. He knew that if she were not so hell bent on marrying him, she might have sensed the real reason for their little joint account. What she didn't know is that marriage to him would make her a family member and the account subject to the taint of insider trading. But given Betsy's knowledge of finance in general, and financial law in particular, he was sure that she never would figure it out.

93

CHAPTER TWENTY

"Asshole," thought Nick, as he hung up the phone. Most of the members of the investment banking side of the firm treated the members of the trading floor as if they were slightly dirty, but to Nick, Smathers was unusually condescending. Smathers' tone had suggested that Nick could not possibly understand what Smathers was up to. Nick was quick to recognize Smathers' style of 'slinging bullshit', and even quicker than most to take offense.

"Schmuck," he added mentally. "That fucker is trading for his own account." As that thought sunk in to one side of the brain, the other side, which functions for most traders on automatic, clicked into action. "He must be doing it because he has inside information. Slimeball."

Now the two brains were meshing. Nick did not have any idea what the inside information was, nor did he want to know, because if he did, he would not be allowed to trade the stock. He was smart enough to avoid any insider trading problems -- if found out, they could turn you from Wall Street partner to taxi driver in no time. But if Nick watched Smathers' actions, then he might be able to deduce the situation, rather than actually know it -- a big difference in the eyes of the Securities and Exchange Commission.

Nick almost called Smathers back to apologize for the sarcasm, but decided that was not required. Instead he called over to the trading desk at Max Adler and Company, where a former colleague was now working.

"Hey, Jimbo. What's the good word."

"Jeez, how long do you think this market can go sideways. I'm getting seasick from all the ups and downs."

"Dunno. I'm even past caring." Not entirely a true statement -- Nick's recent successes were about even with his failures, and he cared. He really cared.

"I got a question for you. You've heard any rumors on the street about USOCO?" That was the second time Jimbo had heard that question that week, the first time was from Max Adler himself.

"No," he answered truthfully -- 'questions' don't count -- only rumors.

"I'm beginning to sense some action, but I don't know why."

"I thought USOCO was your firm's biggest customer."

"It is -- but the investment banking boys don't tell the traders anything, at least not before it's a done deal. Loose lips sink ships."

"Yeah, well, I'll tell you things if you'll tell me things."

"OK. You've got a deal." The two rang off.

Nick checked the action of the stock on the ticker above

his desk. No particular activity. He decided to make his pitch now while things were still quiet. He told his assistant to put in an order for another 400,000 shares. He hoped to God that whatever Smathers was doing that he was right.

USOCO was bought in pieces of 20,000, 50,000 and 100,000 by the Hillman broker on the floor. The stock had only moved another 1/4 of a point. Good work, he thought.

CHAPTER TWENTY ONE

Max Adler actually listened more attentively than he ever appeared to be -- partly because he liked to seem disarming, particularly with really important information, and partly because his mind was already plotting his next move. So it was when Jimbo stopped by his office to pass on his conversation with Hillman Flax. Adler had seemed so uninterested that Jimbo simply shrugged and walked away. Max was already using the information to add to the data bank labeled "USOCO Syndicate" in the left section of his incredible computer-like brain.

Max then called for his brain to do a sort on the information already stored. He came up with the following:

-- USOCO activity up 100,000 shares on the average each trading day. Coincidence?

-- Hillman Flax, their investment bank, asking about rumors. Something must be going on outside USOCO and the bank, otherwise they would already know.

-- Jack McGrory, the USOCO specialist seemed unusually agitated when talking about Matthew Allyn & Co.? Was Allyn doing a lot of purchasing at his post?

-- Matthew Allyn was seen with representative of LeFevre & Cie. Foreign interest in USOCO?

Max picked up the phone and called Jack. It was past four o'clock in the afternoon, the time when the market closes, so Jack would probably be clearing his desk in the upstairs office before going to have some short ones. Max knew if he asked Jack directly about who was trading shares at his post it would be unethical. But Max was way past having to deal with that problem.

"Jack. I've a quick question for you. I'm not holding you up." Max knew that Jack rarely lingered before going for his evening picker-upper.

"No. No. What can I do for you."

"Nothing much. That guy you mentioned the other day at lunch, Whitey Whitehill, you must see him a lot at your post, right. Tell me, uh, is he any good as a broker?"

"Why do you want to know?"

"Uh, someone we know is thinking of taking him aboard their shop."

"Oh. Yeah, he comes all the time. Terrific broker. It always looks like he's only buying a couple hundred and lands up walking away with 100,000. Keeps it close to his vest. Like a goddam poker player."

"Yeah. Well, sounds like our, I mean, their kind of man. Well, thanks. I'll let you get those muscle relaxers."

Max hung up the phone. He was always amazed how easily people let go of information when they weren't asked for it directly. Journalists should learn that skill, he mused.

Max called back to Jimbo. "I'll be giving you some orders for some USOCO purchases tomorrow. Come by my office first thing and I'll give you the numbers and the limits." Jimbo was impressed. When Max 'special handled' the trading, big numbers were always involved. Maybe $50 million. Sometimes more. And Jimbo had thought that Max hadn't even been listening.

Just as Max had intended, Jack figured that Max wanted the information on Whitey for his own shop. Good, thought Jack. The sight of Whitey hanging around his post was beginning to become unnerving. Not that Whitey's absence would make any difference. He knew that even if the floor broker left, the buyer would not stop buying.

CHAPTER TWENTY TWO

In his booth on the floor of the Stock Exchange, Whitey was carefully watching the ticker tape hanging twenty feet above him. The last sale of USOCO had been made at 39 1/2 for 25,000 shares. In general, the market had only been slip sliding through the fall, but it hadn't dampened Wall Street's merger mania, which was still in full swing. The 10:00 AM opening bell had just been rung, and strong activity was present on a number of companies that were the public's favorite takeover contenders.

Matthew Allyn & Co. had certainly prospered in the last four months. Whitey had to give Matt credit -- the relationship with LeFevre appeared solid. The daily purchase orders in USOCO shares had proved to be a real meal ticket. In fact, today's order to buy 200,000 shares was in Matt's mind a further confirmation of LeFevre's faith in their abilities.

Whitey was aware that buying interest in USOCO was spreading as both technicians and traders were increasing their participation in the stock's trading activity. Whitey was well plugged into the institutional mainstream through his various connections on the floor. In particular, he knew that the risk arbitrageurs were beginning to nibble at the stock, meaning that a "story" on USOCO was going around the Street.

As Whitey got close to the USOCO post, it was obvious that the trading was more active than normal. There were about twice as many brokers crowded around the post, yelling their bids and offers to each other. Out of the corner of his eye, Whitey spotted both the Hillman Flax and the Max Adler brokers. Jack McGrory, holding his position book in his hand, looked rather harried. He was trying to control the crowd and make a market in the stock at the same time.

"39 1/2 bid, offered at 40," he yelled above the voices. "50,000 bid for, 50,000 offered."

Whitey could see that the stock was up 1/2 a point from the opening bell -- volume was already heavy. Whitey decided not to diddle around with his order today.

"40 bid, 100,000," he said. With that, Jack sold him the 50,000 he was offering, and Merrill Lynch and Paine Weber filled the rest of the order.

"How's the stock quoted now?" said Whitey.

"40 bid, offered at 40 1/2, 100,000 either way," shouted Jack, to the crowd as much as to Whitey.

Just then the Hillman Flax broker and the Max Adler broker started taking all the stock that was offered at 40 1/2. In just seconds, 300,000 shares had traded up to 41. In this fury, Whitey was only able to buy 25,000 shares -- he sensed that the stock was about to "run away".

"41 bid, offered at 41 1/2," screamed Jack. "100,000 either way."

Whitey wanted to complete the order quickly -- the stock was aleady up 2 points from the opening less than an hour ago.

"41 1/2 for 75,000." Whitey shouted out his bid to all the brokers in the crowd. Quickly Jack and several others filled his order.

Whitey walked over to the nearest floor phone and gave his report to his clerk, Terry. He glanced back and saw that the Hillman Flax and Adler brokers were still in the crowd buying. Other traders started pouring into the crowd -- Whitey knew them all to be representing the major borkerage houses. Apparently the word was spreading that USOCO was around to buy.

Whitey called up to Matt directly. "Matt, we better add on your telex to LeFevre that there is big interest in this stock now. I see all the big players here-- and I don't see any sellers among them. This stock is really going to fly!"

The next morning the "Heard on the Street" column in the Wall Street Journal had the following headline: "Wall Street Rumor Mill Pushes USOCO Stock Up 5 Points. Takeover Stories Not Given Much Credence by Analysts."

Sitting in the back seat of his Mercedes limousine, Andre LeFevre smiled as he read the column in the European edition of the paper. LeFevre and company had accumulated nearly 2% of USOCO -- and still his activities were a mystery to the market. His plan was moving along perfectly.

CHAPTER TWENTY THREE

December, 1985

Since her return to Geneva, Christine had been bothered by the conversation she had had with Matt regarding his dealing with LeFevre. She knew that Matt was being compensated correctly, yet the lack of supporting information at the bank was disturbing. Banks are notorious for having too much paper backing up every transaction, sometimes creating mounds of refuse. In fact, LeFevre & Cie. was particularly proud of the detailed computer systems that Raoul had developed. Why then was there nothing in the system on Matthew Allyn & Company? Could Matt be faced with some major problem down the road because of this?

She considered some possibilities which would explain why Matt's name would not be in the central registry, but none made any real sense. Deep in a zippered section of her purse she kept a folded copy of the telex she had seen in Matt's apartment -- but rarely did she pull it out to look at it. She seemed to be able to think about the situation abstractly, but actually looking at that piece of paper was too confrontational for her -- it meant that she should be taking action -- but she had absolutely no idea where to start.

This afternoon, behind her desk at LeFevre, had been

especially slow. It was the Friday before Christmas, which was on Wednesday, and most of the officers were planning on an early start to their winter vacation. Andre LeFevre was clearing his desk prior to leaving for a week in Gstaad -- his wife had already left to open up the chalet for the season. Most of the bond and currency traders had already left, only the traders that dealt primarily on the American markets remained. They would probably stick it out to five o'clock -- eleven in the morning New York time -- before hitting the road.

Christine had finished the last minute letters, Christmas cards and travel arrangements that are typical for a secretary trying to get her boss out early. LeFevre was just finishing his rounds of the entire staff, giving them his holiday greeting, when he returned to his office to sign the letters and pack up his attache case. As he was leaving he placed the finished correspondence on Christine's desk and gave her a well-practiced smile.

"Miss Evins, I want to give you my warmest wishes for the coming holidays." He reached out to shake her hand.

Christine was slightly abashed. In true European corporate style, LeFevre rarely spoke to her about anything even remotely personal -- even the arrangements for the New York trips were done in a most professional manner, which, for Christine, took the edge of seaminess out of the whole affair. But the truth was that whenever Andre LeFevre came close to her, she was on the verge of a blush. She didn't want to admit it -- like everyone she preferred to think of herself as a sophisticate -- but the combination of the knowledge of his adultery and the closeness of his presence set off in her a soft sexual sensation.

Christine recovered her presence and returned the greeting.

"Thank you very much. And the same to you, and to Madame LeFevre." There was never any acknowledgement of the affair, such as smirks or knowing winks when his wife's name was mentioned. It was as if the whole thing never ever happened, so ingrained was the hypocrisy.

Christine watched him leave. She remembered when Matt had asked her what she thought of Andre and she had answered, "He's very intelligent." If she were entirely truthful, she would have added that if Andre LeFevre ever told her that he was going to divorce his wife, dismiss his mistress and devote himself to her, she would immediately have praised the heavens for having her dream come true. But she was too realistic to dwell on such fantasies and she typed his letters and brought his coffee without the slightest sign of mooniness.

Matt had not been the perfect substitute for LeFevre. She was very fond of him -- he had a far more sensitive and energetic nature than Andre had ever displayed -- but he was no match for Andre's charm, style and aura of wealth. But Matt was not some fantastic dream, he was decidedly real, and she truly enjoyed his company. He had called every Saturday at noon since her return from New York, and she sincerely looked forward to his calls.

Not once during those calls had he mentioned the question of the telex, but she was beginning to feel guilty about her lack of action. As the afternoon became quieter, she decided to give the matter some attention. Besides, without the usual bustle of people in the office, she was bored and a little lonely.

She pulled out the telex and read it carefully. She knew that as far as Matt was concerned, there was no doubt as to its authenticity. Why should he doubt it -- money was always available when payment was due. But why weren't the back office people at LeFevre aware of the trades or of

Matthew Allyn & Co. as a brokerage firm. She knew that all transactions were double checked by their audit department -- they should have been positively able to identify his name.

She was sure that the telex must have come from LeFevre -- the answer back code word was valid. Perhaps one of the traders was secretly buying stock without entering it in the central log. But how would he be able to arrange payment? Was someone also embezzling dollars from their bank account at Morgan Guaranty?

An idea struck her. Every telex machine has a separate identification number -- perhaps if she could discover which machine in the bank sent the telex, she could track down who typed it in. She asked the switchboard operator to cover the incoming telephone calls, and went down to the main trading room. Off to one side were all the telex machines, six in a row, which handled all incoming and outgoing messages. Two operators normally did all of the inputting -- but both had left early with the other traders, leaving only the account reconciliation clerk there to handle the occasional late day outgoing message.

Christine checked the carbon copies of the messages that the machine automatically produces. Of all the machines, not one machine number even came close to the number on her copy. Apparently all six had been purchased at the same time, because the machines had very similar numbers. The machine she was looking for was from a completely different series of numbers.

"Excuse me, may I ask if these telex machines are used to send messages to stockbrokers confirming our trading transactions?"

The reconcilation clerk looked up -- he had expected to hear something like 'Merry Christmas', not a question about telex machines.

"These are the only ones we use," he replied.

Christine was bewildered. Now it appeared that the telex did not even emerge from the bank.

"Why do you ask?" said the clerk, with uncommon curiosity for a Swiss bank employee.

Christine didn't know what to say. "Just curious." The answer couldn't have sounded more stupid, thought Christine.

"Oh," replied the clerk. "Because there is another machine, you know."

"There is? Why did you say these were the only ones."

"I didn't. I said these were the only ones we use. We don't use the other one -- it's just for emergencies."

Christine felt silly. "Where is it," she ventured, wondering if she were phrasing this question correctly.

"In a closet in Mr. Hengler's office."

"Oh. Thank you." Christine looked up. She could see Raoul sitting behind the glass partition -- the door was closed and he was apparently completely absorbed in reviewing the days work. Should she ask to see the machine, she wondered. Would Raoul question why she was asking? It occurred to her that if Raoul were sending the telex then there shouldn't be any cause for concern -- after all he was the head trader and bookkeeper. But still, why weren't the trades being logged? She was very confused.

She went to his office. Without knocking, she entered his office. He had apparently not seen her approach, for he his office. He had apparently not seen her approach, for he was startled by her appearance.

"Why didn't you knock?" he demanded angrily. He started to put his arm over some of his paperwork as if to hide it from her view.

"I don't know."

"You shouldn't come in without knocking. What do you want?"

His annoyance had prevented her from advancing much closer than the doorway. "I only wanted to wish you Merry Christmas", she stammered, deciding to pursue the matter of the telex machine some other time.

Raoul softened. "Yes, thank you very much. And the same to you. Now please go away. I am very busy."

Christine backed away, visibly shakened. Why was he so rude, she wondered. What had she interrupted?

CHAPTER TWENTY FOUR

It was Christmas Eve. The New York Stock Exchange never closed for trading except under extreme duress, such as weekends and legal holidays. It even opened for trading now on Presidential election days, and it was actively discussing longer hours. Commission income was too much for Wall Street to give up simply to enjoy a day without work.

The day before Christmas is one of the slowest on the Street. The roads leaving the city were jammed starting in the early afternoon. The snow had started to fall and the atmosphere was filled with both annoyance and anticicpation of the holiday period ahead.

At Matthew Allyn & Co., the problem was that if one too many people left the office early there would be no one remaining to man the store. And that is what Matt and Whitey considered the firm to be -- a candy store that had to stay open every day, while the proprietors rang the cash register with the daily receipts. There was no doubt between Matt and Whitey that this had been their year to ring the register.

Matt and Whitey, with no particular place to rush off to, were alone in the office after the close. Whitey, who had been shooting rubber bands aimlessly into the air, said, "You know Matt, I don't understand what LeFevre is up to. They've bought about 15 million shares of USOCO and I can't tell what the object is."

"Maybe the object will be to start a selling program in the stock after the new year," said Matt. "Which is okay by me because the commissions will be just as good for us on the sell side as on the buy side."

"Well, that would make sense," said Whitey, "the stock has gone up 15 points and that's probably as far as it's going to go."

Matt did some quick mental calculations. They had been buying USOCO stock for the past five months at the general rate of about 100,000 shares per day. That worked out at a commisssion rate of four cents per share to four thousand dollars per day or $80,000 per month. It had meant an additional $400,000 for the firm in the past five months. It had certainly made the difference between a very poor and a very good year.

"We really stepped into some shit with this one, didn't we?" said Matt. "I hope it never ends."

"Well, it'll be at least another $400,000 in commissions when they start selling that stuff. Christ, that's $800,000 in total income. Thank you, God!"

"Yeah. And all for being in the right place at the right time."

"Better lucky than smart, I always say," said Whitey.

"You know, Horst has been buying a lot of shares for his own account -- he started back when USOCO was still $34 a share. I guess LeFevre told him to get in quick."

110

"Somthing must be going on," said Whitey, "Horst is really a trader and not an investor. He's usually in for the short term only. I can't believe he hasn't sold out his position yet. He's sitting on a profit of about $500,000. That's a pretty good piece of change by anyone's standard."

"Well, it could be that this stock isn't finished yet. Maybe there's a takeover in the works after all".

Matt found that hard to believe even as he said it. USOCO was just too big to become someone else's plum. Still, LeFevre must be holding on to his now gargantuan position for a specific reason. And that reason could only be based on the greed factor. He obviously thought that there was more blood to be sucked from the USOCO stone before it went dry.

"Matt, let's drink to the new year. I think we have a decent bottle of wine kicking around that must have been a gift from one of our more generous customers this Christmas."

Whitey found a bottle of some 1979 Bordeaux and poured out two glasses.

"Here's to us", toasted Matt. "May we always be smart. And failing that, may we always be even luckier."

They both drank heartily.

As Matt put his empty glass down on his desk, his thoughts turned to Christine. For a Christmas gift, he had sent her pearl earrings to match the necklace she was wearing the first day he met her. A bit too traditional, he had decided, but he couldn't come up with a better idea. He wondered if she had opened it or if she was saving it for Christmas Day. He wondered if she had made any progress on finding out why their name was so secret within LeFevre

& Cie. He wondered if she loved him.

At the same time, Max Adler was leaning back in his leather chair in his Park Avenue office. As dusk neared, the lights of the city, especially resplendent during Christmas time, presented a spectacular view before him. The traditions of Christmas meant little to him, but he savored the glow. He smiled contentedly. The year had been good.

He had smelled the promise of takeover of USOCO. The stock acted too well. Right now it was in a holding pattern for the end of the year, but he expected that it would move again in January. He had gotten together twenty five members of a syndicate, and they had anted up $100,000,000 among them to buy the stock on Max's suggestion alone. Max had that kind of clout.

The phone rang. It was Marty Fishbein, a very successful textile converter, and one of Max's earliest investors.

"Happy Chanukah, Max."

"Same to you, Marty." Max didn't even know when Chanukah fell that year.

"Max, you know, I've been thinking. I see that we have already made a pretty penny on our USOCO position. The stock seems to be a little quiet right now. Do you think we should start selling."

"Marty -- I love you. But you make blue jeans, I'll trade stocks."

"Max, Max. I'm not telling you what to do. God knows you've turned me from a poor slob to a rich one. But I have bad feelings about this. It just doesn't seem right."

"What doesn't seem right?"

"You know, this whole thing about takeovers. USOCO's too big to be taken over."

"I dunno about that, Marty. My hunch says they are. We're going to play this one out further. I think the fireworks are yet to come."

"Okay, Max. You're the doctor. But I hope you got the right prescription on this one."

Jon Smathers rolled off Betsy and stared up at the ceiling. He had taken the week off and was home visiting his parents in Brookline. Betsy had made lunch at her Back Bay apartment, close to the Museum of Fine Arts where she was an assistant curator in the American Folk Art Department. Her salary was barely adequate -- but it was amply supplemented by the income from her trust fund.

Smathers thought to himself that the USOCO options that Betsy had purchased for them had almost doubled by now. But he wasn't going to sell. Not yet -- he could tell that there was real action to come before this story was over.

Besides, if he was going to maintain his memberships in his polo clubs, mainly Piping Rock out on Long Island, he would need a big hit in the market. Besides, he had a bid on two polo ponies, the minimum for any player, he was thinking of buying, and they would need a lot of hay. He smiled to himself. He needed to make bread to buy hay.

"Come on Bets, get that beautiful ass of yours in gear. We've got to hurry if we're going to get to your parents house in time for the roast duck".

Nick Bianco was also in the sack in the early afternoon this Chrismas Eve. But with Carol, his bought and paid for lover, not his wife. That would be later that evening. The pleasure for Nick, however, would only be now, later would be his husbandly duty. He was a good husband, even though his wife saw through him as if he was made of lucite. She was no dummy -- Nick was a conscientious father and a better provider -- he never quarreled no matter how much money she spent.

Nick had done a masterful job of trading for Hillman Flax during the past two months. The play in USOCO stock had pulled the trading year out of the fire for him. The stock had given him a couple million extra dollars of trading profit for the department. But something nagged at his unconscious. He had been in the business so long that anything out of the ordinary sent warning bells clanging in his mind. He too, like Max Adler, Jonathan Smathers, Matt and Whitey, Jack McGrory, smelled bigger game as far as the USOCO stock was concerned.

Carol came back from the bathroom. She looked terrific, Nick thought, but that's how mistresses are supposed to look. Otherwise they might as well be wives.

"Nicky, honey, we've still got some more time before you got to go. Why don't we do it again special for the holiday," she said with an obvious pleading look. Nick wondered how much was real, and how much was done to

114

assure the constant flow of dollars he sent her each month.

Nick who had turned on the the ticker tape on the cable TV channel while she was in the bathroom, acquiesced, with some reluctance. He turned down the volume but kept himself positioned to see the screen.

Making money is really more exciting than fucking, he thought.

CHAPTER TWENTY FIVE

The day after Christmas is generally anticlimactic in any locale, but for Christine there was a special sense of what the German's call 'weltschmertz', loosely translated as world weariness. Several emotions seemed to be colliding. First was the quietness of the holidays, which she spent at her parent's weekend chalet in Grindelwald. That left in her a longing for more excitement, more interaction.

The second was her involvement with Matt. He had sent her a gift -- from the size and the weight of the box it seemed like a stuffed toy animal. So she waited to open it on Christmas Day at her parent's place, a mistake, because on the teddy bear's ears were pearl earrings. She was delighted -- none of the Swiss men she had been going with had that kind of whimsey. They would not invest money into a relationship unless they were both 'serious'. But because of that her parents read something into the situation and insisted on knowing every detail of the man who was so generous. That embarrassment was still present when Matt phoned her at the chalet. Her parents were within hearing range -- she was caught between wanting to gush over the gift to please Matt and to act restrained to diminish her parent's concern. The result was unsatisfying to all parties.

The third was her nagging concern about the Matthew

Allyn and LeFevre business. One voice in her head said to forget the matter, another said to be diligent -- for Matt's sake. She decided the best course would be to silence both voices by attempting to only determine why the telexes were so secret. After that she would drop the matter.

She flipped through several of the customers' files sitting on her desk. Not one portfolio summary showed any holdings in USOCO. Perhaps the accumulation is all for one customer. But which one -- to her knowledge there was no customer that could afford such a large purchase. Whitey had hinted at a Middle Eastern contact -- no Arabs had come into the bank for the last two years. LeFevre simply had no contacts in that part of the world.

The day dragged by. By five, the employees who had not taken the week off were out the door. Only the guards remained. With no particularly well thought out tactic in mind, Christine had decided to take another look for the telex machine in Raoul's office. After all, even if she did succeed in proving that that machine was used for the transactions, what conclusions could be drawn. None, except that perhaps Raoul was sending the telexes, or perhaps he wasn't.

She went down to the trading room -- empty except for a cleaning person making rounds in the far corner. She looked in Raoul's office. No one was there. Raoul almost never took a vacation -- leaving at five on the nose was the closest he came to taking time off. She tried the handle on the door -- not surprisingly it was locked. Locking was part of a Swiss tradition -- locked doors, locked credenzas, locked files, locked liqour cabinets -- even casual home furniture were built with with locking mechanisms.

Christine decided to pursue the cause. The emptiness of the office gave her courage -- if she thought she could be spotted she would not have gone on. She went down to the

117

night guard on the main floor. Since she often stayed late, she knew him quite well. Besides, he was a German speaking Swiss, who were a minortiy group in French speaking Geneva. She had always made it a point to speak Switzerdeutsch to him, the German dialect, which he seemed to truly appreciate.

"Oh, Herr Ringgli, I have a little problem."

"Oh, Miss Evins, hopefully we can help you with it." He gave Christine a broad fatherly smile. He was to Christine the epitome of the little Swiss winemaker.

"You probably can -- you see I left some correspondence with Mr. Hengler, and now he has gone. Mr. LeFevre called about those papers, but they are locked in Mr. Hengler's office. Do you have the key to that room?"

"Of course I do. Such a simple problem. I'll get them for you right away." The old man went over to a wall safe, which he opened with a key on his belt. On the inside section of the safe door hung a number of keys, each separately marked, apparently duplicates for all the keys in the building. Ringgli removed one of the sets, which contained three keys of different sizes.

"Oh, that's wonderful. I'll return them right away."

"But take your time. I'll be here all evening."

Christine smiled. Sometimes things went quite smoothly.

Christine returned to the trading room. The cleaning person was still there, having moved closer to the bank of offices nearer to Hengler's. Christine smiled at him, as if to suggest that nothing was amiss, and used the largest key to open Hengler's door. In the back was a closet, also locked.

The middle size key fit that lock. Inside was the telex machine and two banks of filing cabinets. Christine turned her attention to the carbons in the back of the machine. By now she was familiar with the number on her own copy and she recognized it immediately as the same as the machine's.

Now her curiosity had not been sated, but rather intensified. She pulled at the cabinet drawers -- locked, of course. She tried the third key. It did not fit. Why wasn't it among the bank's masters. Perhaps it was in Raoul's desk. She used the third key which was good to open the top drawer. In the cubbyhole reserved for keys, paper clips and assorted matter there was indeed another set of keys.

She pulled them out and went back to the filing cabinets. She unlocked the first set and opened the top drawer. In there were customers' records, kept in separate manila files by name. She peered in one file -- inside were portfolio ledgers, except rather than done in the computer format she was used to, they were made up by hand. She opened some other drawers. The same thing. Christine felt ridiculous. What had she been expecting to see -- secrets of the Swiss Army's mountain missile sites?

Christine locked all the files, and closed the closet door. Just as she was locking that up, she heard a voice, Raoul's, boom behind her.

"I have a bone to pick with you," he was saying angrily. Christine stiffened -- she felt the blood rushing to her face. She looked out of the office's partition. Raoul was directly outside, but standing with his back to her. He was talking to the cleaning person, not to her. He must not have left for the day, but only gone out for supper. Apparently he had not even seen her. She quickly ducked behind the desk.

Raoul was complaining to the cleaning person that he had thrown out some important papers. The cleaning person

119

was protesting, stating that he only threw out what was lying on the floor. They went over to the spot across the room where the disputed event took place. Christine peered up from behind the desk. Raoul was out of view. She pulled open the drawer, stuck the keys back in, and locked up the desk. Now to get out of the office.

She crawled on the floor, carefully opened the door, and snuck out. Raoul was out of sight behind the banks of monitors and telephone boards. She debated whether to attempt to relock the door. She decided it was worth the risk -- Raoul would certainly have remembered locking it, and would have been suspicious if the door had been open now. Angling the key into the lock was more arduous than expected -- one is used to pressing directly onto a key rather than from below to turn it. Although it seemed endless to her, she succeeded in turning the lock in ten seconds.

In the background, she could still hear Raoul arguing with the cleaning person. She stayed low, wandering around he circumference of the trading banks until she came to a part of the room that was furthest from the both Raoul and his office. She waited until the arguing stopped and he returned to his office. She then completed the rest of her maneuver, still on her hands and knees, until she reached the desks nearest the door. If she continued crawling, she would have decidedly looked suspicious to the cleaning person, whose line of sight she would have had to cross. She peered towards Raoul's office, but could not see him from her position. She decided to make a go for it -- she stood up and raced through the door.

When in the outside hall, she went to the fire stairwell and ran up the stairs back to her own office. She sat behind her desk for five minutes, just long enough to gain composure. She doubted that Raoul had seen her -- but she decided not to stay around any longer. She closed up her own office for the evening, and rushed out using the main stairwell instead of the creaky old elevator. She returned the keys to Ringgli, and walked home along the river.

Christine was mistaken about Raoul -- he had seen her leave the office. He considered running after her, but instead got up to check the office. Everything looked to be in its proper place. He opened his top desk drawer. His keys were in the well, but in a strangely askew fashion. Is that how he left them? He couldn't remember. He went over to the window to watch. He was sure that he would see her leaving the building shortly. He was not mistaken. She was walking with long strides towards the lake. Raoul looked to see if she were carrying any files. Apparently not. But nonetheless, she would have to be carefully watched from now on.

CHAPTER TWENTY SIX

Christine sat in bed sipping a cognac. She was still shaken from the experience. Clearly, she was not cut out to be a spy -- simple adventures such as this one were enough to lay her low for the entire evening. She tried making sense of what she saw -- but nothing amounted to anything. A telex machine in a back office, files of customers' portfolios -- so what? What is so odd about seeing those in the head trader's office?

Instead of calming her, the cognac only heightened her fears. She dreaded to think of what might have occurred if Raoul had seen her in his office -- fast action thinking was not her forte. It passed through her mind that he might have noticed her leaving the main room, but she dismissed that as unlikely. Thoughts swirled in her head, without making any coherent pattern. Eventually, out of mental exhaustion and the desire to escape, she fell asleep.

At three o'clock she woke, her mind instantly alert. The thought that eluded her before came clearly to mind. There was no reason for Raoul to make hand notations of the customers' accounts -- everything was done by computer. So all the records would be double effort, unless he was manipulating the computer imput. Christine started to shake.

Was it a case of imagination gone wild? Was she going crazy?

She picked up her private telephone book and looked up a number. She then dialed thirteen digits.

Matt answered the phone in his apartment -- it was only nine o'clock in New York.

"Matt, this is Christine."

"Christine, what are you doing calling me so late? Did you suddenly miss me?"

"Matt, listen. I have something to tell you."

Matt listened to her whole story. If what she was implying were true, then Raoul might be embezzling a fortune. This was something that Matt didn't want to know. He didn't want to be on the fool's end again.

"Christine, wait a minute, you have forgotten one thing. Those telexes are not just coming from Raoul -- they are signed by Andre. And I'm sure that Andre LeFevre has authorized this whole buy program. In fact, Andre made it quite clear to me that that was how they wanted to do it. You're imagining things. You're picking on Raoul because he seems so sinister. He is probably just a very conscientous person keeping a double set of files for his personal use. So relax."

Christine did not respond right away. "You're probably right. I'm just a silly secretary looking for adventure. Do you forgive me?"

Matt smiled. The role of being the knight savior appealed to him. "Of course, I do. And I don't think of you as silly -- you're too smart. Now you get the rest of your sleep, and I'll call you in the office in the afternoon."

"Yes, okay. No, wait. Not at the office. Call me tomorrow evening, in the apartment. It's more private that way."

"You've got it."

Christine hung up the phone. She wanted to tell Matt that she was scared -- but was afraid of appearing even sillier. She crawled back into bed and slept fitfully.

CHAPTER TWENTY SEVEN

On New Year's Eve, Horst Meyer sat near the fireplace in the living room of Andre LeFevre's chalet in Gstaad. They had finished an afternoon of skiing, without his girlfriend or Andre's wife, who had headed into town together to do shopping and to prepare for the evening's party. Several neighbors were invited for midnight supper, a la Suisse, meaning it would be simple fare, including the more hearty delicacies, such as bundnerfleisch, thin dried smoked beef, raclette, cheese grilled directly over an open fire, rosti, fried grated potates, and the local wines, like dole and fendant. At midnight there would be plenty of Taitinger and schnapps.

Andre entered the room with several bottles of the fendant and some bar glasses. His mood was already turning jovial -- the skiing had been more challenging and exciting because the ladies were not along. In addition, Andre had invited one of the female ski instructors with whom he was anticipating having an affair. Andre poured the wine into an especially large tumbler and handed it to Horst. Horst gave Andre a questioning look.

"Horst, I'm in such an expansive mood that I have decided to dispense with the formalities of drinking. In short, I'm ready to drink. So let's unwind a bit while the ladies are occupied. Anyway, it's the only time we'll be able to catch up on old times alone -- someone else is bound to be around us for the rest of the weekend."

"Things must be going very well at the firm. You know, this is the first time I've really seen you completely relaxed since your father died."

"Really. Horst, does it show that much? But you're right. This is the first time I've felt comfortable running the bank."

"Then you must be making some very good decisions." Horst was thinking of his own portfolio, which had ended the year to mixed reviews.

"Oh, I have. You must know, Horst, that I, eh, I mean, one of my clients is behind the USOCO stock rally."

Horst was surprised. On Andre's suggestion some months ago, Horst had bought 50,000 shares for the firm. But he had failed to make the connection between the tip and the takeover stories.

"You mean all that play on the stock is coming from your house."

"Well, not all of it. Just in the beginning. Now others are in on it, which is exactly what we had hoped for."

"Well, it certainly has done wonders for the stock's price. I bought it at $35. Right now it is selling at $45. In fact, I was thinking of selling right after the year end."

"Selling. Don't be a fool. There is plenty of play in that stock yet."

"But you never know. It can go down."

"But it won't."

"How do you know? Are you going to be doing some more buying?"

Andre smiled. "Oh, I expect to be doing a lot more than just buying. You see, I have plan. For my client, that is. I expect that the price will go to at least 55, maybe even 60, before it is over."

"That would take a lot of buying. And only a very rich person could afford to corner the USOCO stock."

"Arabs are reputed to be very rich," replied Andre, not really answering the question. "You know, I shouldn't be telling you this. But you should take advantage of this information."

Horst thought for a moment. He knew his firm's capital to be fully invested at the end of the year. And he already tied up all his extra funds in the 50,000 USOCO, which cost him $1,750,000. His father still ran the firm and right now was not very keen on the American stock market. He was very conservative, and rarely did a deal based on rumor. But of course, this was not exactly rumor. Maybe, he could talk his father into it.

"You know, Andre, my father is just like yours was -- he stills runs the firm as if he were the only person there. He gives me very little of my own decision authority -- everything else must go through him. And right now he has been getting out of American stocks. So, I don't know."

"Well, don't come for a visit here at Easter crying in your German beer because you didn't follow my advice. This is a guaranteed deal."

Just then the doorbell rang. "Must be the first of the guests," said Andre. "Well, think about it. You can't lose."

The guest entered the room. Andre made the introductions. "Herr Garweiler, I would like you to meet Horst Meyer, of Meyer and Sohne in Dusseldorf."

"I am extremely pleased to meet you," said Horst sincerely. Hans Garweiler was the renowned head of the Swiss Central Bank, and a leading spokesman for international banking and financial matters.

"I am pleased to be here," replied Garweiler. "I am lucky to have Andre as my neighbor. Then I know he has to invite me to his parties, or I will complain to the police about the noise."

Horst laughed at Garweiler's typically Swiss humor. "But really are you neighbors? Andre never mentioned it before."

"Well, it is really only our little joke. You see, my chalet's property is back to back with LeFevre's, even though you cannot really cross from one side to the other. I must actually go all the way down my road to the main street, and then up another to reach his house." Garweiler went on to describe his chalet and its location to the mountain in fine detail.

Horst was following the conversation, but just barely. His mind was still on the discussion about the USOCO stock. Horst sighed. The best tip he'd ever receive and he couldn't do a thing. Or could he? He began to concoct a plan in his head. Something that would prove to his father that he, too, could make money for the bank.

CHAPTER TWENTY EIGHT

Jack McGrory was not in the mood for New Year's Eve partying. The local chapter of the Sons of Hibernia were throwing a dinner dance at the Plaza, which Jack and his wife attended faithfully every year. But this year, Jack would have just as soon stayed home with a bottle of Irish.

The firm was losing money. Doing so was not completely unheard of in the stockmarket. Specialists firms do lose money when the market collapses -- the firms are stuck with stock noboby wants -- one or two have been even known to close their doors. Occasionally, they lose money during sharp market upturns, but much less frequently, mainly because wild bull rallies happen much less frequently than free fall declines.

The simple truth was that Jack had not been prepared for the continuous rally that was overwhelming the USOCO stock. In particular, the stock seemed to be gathering more volume as the stories of a takeover persisted. Since he culd not believe that anyone would attempt to take over the company, he could not believe that anyone else would fall for the rumor. But every day he saw a larger crowd around his post, and they were all buyers. And as he continued to provide them with stock, he had to be short of USOCO stock himself. That meant he continully had to buy it back to cover his position at higher prices. So far this rumor about USOCO had cost the firm over $12,000,000.

Jack was not worried about going out of business -- at least not yet. But losing money consistently was decidedly not fun. He had no one to answer to -- after all he was the senior partner -- but he didn't want to have to leave the company as a loser. And the younger partners would certainly edge him out if this situation continued.

Unfortunately, he knew there was no way to stop it. If buyers lose heart in the takeover rumor, things might actually get worse. Sellers would start showing up at his post, and he would have to buy the shares into his own inventory, all the while watching the price decline. The only hope was that for some reason there would be an official halt in the trading of the stock, which would allow Jack to reset the price at a level that would be favorable to the firm. Then the sellers would start coming in. But that was a slim chance.

People were approaching Jack all evening in various states of inebriation wishing him a Happy New Year. Jack wondered if he were as unappealing as they were when he drank. His wife was giving the nod that she wanted to dance. Jack dutifully stood up to oblige. He checked his watch. Only 10:30. Another two hours before he could even suggest going home.

He had never felt so old.

Herbert Kramer, the CEO of USOCO, was also feeling old. He was pushing arugula salad, which he hated, around in its bowl at a New Year's dinner party being held by the head of the Houston Arts Council. Most of the conversation involved some new museum in the plans, which was really his wife's province. Kramer was off the hook as far as conversation was concerned, but he could not leave the table, which was his only real wish. He considered begging off with a headache, but rejected that as being too feminine.

Kramer began thinking about USOCO. The takeover rumor persisted, but he could not get at the source of it. Owen Perry had told him that some company named Monblank, which he knew was a nominee name, was accumulating shares, but nothing made any sense. After some delibration, Perry had submitted a list of domestic names which might be the buyers, but all of them were oil companes, and would be running up against anti-trust laws. That meant that Monblank might represent foreign interests.

Kramer downed some wine. The thought of a takeover had always seemed so remote to him. It was never discussed at management meetings, never raised as an issue before the Board. It never really existed in their scope of reality.

Kramer now was dogged by fear. Fear that the acquiring company was for real --fear that the buyer woud want to dump him. Even worse, if the bidder were an Arab, he had to leave for sure. Even if they wanted him to stay, highly unlikely as it sounded, he would go. He wouldn't have been able to tolerate reporting to Arabs. The thought made Kramer shudder.

His wife nudged him. "What's wrong?" she whispered. "Are you all right? You haven't eaten anything."

"Mmm, mmm." He had not told his wife of his fears. It sounded so absurd that he felt silly for being so scared. Anyway, she probably would have been for it -- she had been after him for early retirement for several years.

He thought of his pension plan. Certainly ample, but it did not cover early retirements or forced withdrawals. He decided to get the compensation department together right after the holidays to discuss including a large lump sum payment to be made to senior officers who were terminated after a takeover. 'Golden Parachutes" they are called.

Kramer was starting to get agitated. Goddam Arabs, he thought. What fucking right do they have to take over our oil companies? They should stick to pushing camels' asses around deserts where they belong. Goddam bastards. Stinking mother fuckers!

Suddenly he felt a sharp jab in this thigh. "Herbert," his wife said, in as a low a voice as would sound commanding, "what is going on? Now you are talking to yourself."

CHAPTER TWENTY NINE

After talking to Matt, who again reassured her that she was exaggerating her concerns, Christine put the matter of the customers' files in the back of her mind. In reality, the enormity of the possibilities it suggested were too much for her to cope with -- if Raoul were duplicating files, it could only suggest embezzlement, which could prove to be a great blow to the bank. On the other hand, if, as Matt suggested, he were merely being conscientious, then Christine would be seriously at fault if she accused him of anything else. She wanted to exonerate Raoul -- but for her sake, not his. She didn't particularly like him, but she didn't want this problem to be nagging at her conscience any longer. But she didn't know how to do that without informing on him to someone else.

She finally decided the only solution was to get a closer look at the files herself and make some comparisons. If they conformed to the computer files, obviously he was only maintaining copies for his own use. But as they were under lock and key, and asking for the key from Herr Ringgli a second time would undoubtedly arouse even his suspicion. She thought about it for a long time.

By the beginning of February, she had a plan. She started working later hours, practically every night. She also had a discussion with the cleaning person, the one who had been so soundly reprimanded by Raoul, about the hours Raoul usually leaves for his dinner break. She visited some locksmiths in the city regarding duplicate keys. Then she put her plan in action.

One afternoon, she received at the office a very large box from a nearby florist. After the usual office compliments, in which she declined to state who the admirer was, she placed the flowers in a large vase full of water. That evening, after most of the staff had left, she brought the vase down to the ground floor.

"Oh, Herr Ringgli, I just wondered if you would do me a simple favor. These flowers came for me today, but they are so large that they overwhelm my desk, and I have a pile of work yet to do. Would you hold them on your desk until I leave this evening."

"It would be my pleasure," said the old man in his most gracious tone.

"You are so kind. Thank you." Christine started to put the vase down, but as she did, she seemed to trip over her own feet, because she suddenly lurched forward, splashing the contents on the guard in front of her.

"Oh, Herr Ringgli, I spilled water on your coat. Oh, dear."

"It's nothing, it's just water."

"No, it's terrible. The jacket is all wet."

"It'll dry. Don't worry."

"I have a better idea. I'll put my hair dryer to it. I have a small one upstairs. It'll dry in no time."

"Not necessary."

"Yes, yes. I insist. Quickly, take your jacket off. I'll be finished before you know it."

The guard, feeling that it was easier to comply than to argue, handed over the jacket. Christine took the jacket to the third floor bathroom, where she already had her hair dryer out and waiting. She also had waiting on the sink shelf several small wax balls, which she had flattened with the palm of her hand. As she trained the stream of air onto the wet spot, she fished in the jacket for the guard's master keys. She carefully made impressions in the wax of three keys on the chain-- one key was for the front door, one was for the automatic alarm system, and one was for the key box.

After the appropriate amount of drying had been done, she rushed back with the jacket. The old guard was clearly relieved to be back in uniform -- as if he were powerless only being in shirtsleeves. Christine had been careful to clean off all the wax from the keys and to replace them in the correct pocket -- which, out of habit, was the first place he checked after he put the jacket back on. Apparently he seemed satisfied that nothing was amiss, and Christine, pleased with the job she had done, returned to her desk.

Several evenings later Christine placed a call to Ringgli from a room on the ground level, but out of Renggli's view.

"Herr Ringgli. This is Christine Evins. I am hearing a very strange noise coming from the floor above me. In the accounting department. I called up there by phone, but there was no answer. Do you think I should go there by myself to check it out."

"No, no, you stay where you are -- I'll go. You stay by your desk."

Ringgli locked his desk, doubled checked the front door and went upstairs by the elevator. Christine slipped out from her hiding place, went to the key box, opened it with one of the keys she had had the locksmith make from the wax molds, and made some more impressions. After finishing, she went back to her office using the stairwell. She arrived in time to hear her phone starting to ring.

"Yes, Herr Ringgli," she said with what she believed to be the correct amount of worry in her voice.

"I looked into the matter for you -- but I think you are hearing things. There was nothing going on in that room. In fact it was tight as a drum."

"Oh, maybe it was just the cleaning people. I'm so sorry to bother you. But you've made me feel much better."

"That's what I'm here for. Call me if you hear that noise again. Good-by."

Christine smiled. She was beginning to feel like quite an expert burglar.

The next week she made her move. She waited in an alcove near the main trading room at the time the cleaning person indicated Raoul usually leaves for dinner. After she saw him go out, she entered his office with the new set of keys, took the ones for the filing cabinet from his desk, and carefully removed three specific files. She knew she was running the risk of the cleaning person seeing her, but she doubted that he actually would approach Raoul with any information after the way he had been treated. Besides she was moving with considerably more speed and confidence than the last time, and even had an excuse ready, albeit a weak one, should Raoul suddenly return. She carefully made duplicates of everything in the files on the departments Xerox machine, and returned the originals to Raoul's office.

At her desk she compared the notes in Raoul's files with the one with the same customers' names that she retrieved frm central files. If they compared line for line -- well, she would have wasted 100 Swiss francs of her own money on flowers and keys made from molds -- but she would sleep considerably more soundly.

But the contents of the files didn't match. The hand written files all showed losses from investments, the computer generated files all showed gains. The differences in some case were small, in other cases large. Christine gasped -- Raoul must be systematically looting the bank. Despite the fact that she expected to find evidence of wrongdoing, actually seeing it with her own eyes stunned her. She sat behind her desk for several minutes just staring. She wanted to run away -- figuratively, if not literally -- rather than accepting the possibility of a thief among the bank staff.

She spent the rest of the evening at home reviewing how she was going to report her findings to Andre LeFevre. She knew that the method she had used to retrieve the information was in itself suspect, and that she might come under attack in some fashion. She had a hard time falling asleep, which caused her to oversleep in the morning. By the time she got to the bank, Andre LeFevre had already arrived.

She organized her papers and went to knock on Andre's door. Inside she could hear him talking, apparently on the phone, since there was no voice responding to his questions. She looked at her own desk phone panel, but could see none of the lights lit up. She listened more intently, ostensively waiting for him to finish his conversation before entering.

"Are these numbers correct now?" she heard. "All right, then run the computer listing again. Yes, for the quarter end too, we want to look good for the directors. Very good. Okay. Yes, I'm watching Christine. Don't worry. Okay.

137

Bye."

Christine moved back from the door. Suddenly she was very confused. The conversation with Andre that she had so carefully rehearsed last night dissolved in her thoughts. She went back to her desk and slowly sat down, placing the papers she was carrying in the drawer.

Andre LeFevre peered out of his office.

"Oh, Miss Evins, you are here. Could you please bring me a cafe filtre? Thank you."

Christine watched him close his office doors. Unable to control her emotion, she jumped out of her chair and ran to the ladies' room. There she entered a stall, locked it behind her and started to sob. After fifteen minutes she was more in control, returned to her desk and arranged for the coffee. She would tough out the day until she could talk to Matt that evening. It occurred to her that without him, she would be facing this all alone.

CHAPTER THIRTY

Andre reached into the right breast pocket of his Savile Row suit and pulled out his small black leather address book. George Hendricks, the LeFevre account manager at Hillman Flax he had contacted, had conveniently provided him with Herbert Kramer's private telephone number at home. He drew a deep breath and began to dial on the private line. He stopped and put down the phone. This was a critical moment, and he was losing his nerve. He reached into the bottom drawer of his desk, where he kept a secret stash of hazlenut chocolate bars, pulled one out, ate it, and returned the empty wrapper to his drawer.

Satiated and buoyed, he picked up the phone and dialed Kramers's number again. It would be just seven in the morning in Houston and he wanted to catch a still sleepy Kramer. The advantage of a surprise call from a stranger at such an early hour would surely put Kramer off guard. Andre liked that -- he always looked to have a competitive edge in business negotiations or in this case, confrontation.

The phone rang only once before a voice answered.

"Hello."

"Mr. Kramer. I'm so sorry to call you at such an early hour. This is Andre LeFevre, Managing Director of LeFevre & Cie in Geneva. George Hendricks at Hillman Flax, whom I'm sure you know, was kind enough to provide me with your home phone number.

"I wanted to call you regarding a very confidential matter. It was best to call you at home, away from nosy switchboard operators at your office."

"Well, Mister LeFevre, what can I do for you," Kramer replied. He had never heard of LeFevre & Cie., and he hoped this wasn't just a crank call.

"Mr. Kramer. You're aware, I'm sure, of the strong activity in your stock for the past six months. What you may not know is that LeFevre & Cie. has been the major buyer for some of our foreign clients. You might be particularly be familiar with purchases under the name Monblank handled through a small brokerage firm in New York, Matthew Allyn & Co."

"Yes. We're aware of these matters, Mister LeFevre. But if you have something to tell me shouldn't you do it through our mutual relationship at Hillman Flax?" replied a now fully awake Kramer.

"What I have to say is best kept close to both our vests. I wish to do it in private and in person. Could you meet me this weekend in London."

"What's wrong with Houston?" asked Kramer.

"I think we would both be more inconspicuous in London. This is not the type of story you would like anyone speculating on -- especially with the rumor mill so active these days about anything relating to USOCO."

The CEO of USOCO was a very busy man, and not used to being told what to do and where to go. But something within him said that this was not a time to let his ego rule. "I'll be there, Mr. LeFevre. When and where?"

"I'll be staying at the Connaught. Could you come to my suite at 9 o'clock Saturday morning?"

"Very well. I'll see you then," said Kramer curtly as he hung up the phone.

Andre let out a deep breath, closed his eyes and smiled as he heard the click from across the Atlantic. He picked up the phone and dialed Raoul's number. "Okay." he said, as if speaking in code. "The game begins in earnest now."

Over the intercom, he gave Christine instructions to make travel arrangements for a trip to London for himself starting the next day, and for Mr. Hengler for the weekend. Having no other appointments on his caladar, he left for the afternoon. In his mind he had already put in a good day's work.

CHAPTER THIRTY ONE

Herb Kramer immediately called Owen Perry, who was just about to leave for his morning jog. Owen's blood pressure jumped when he heard Kramer's voice -- his first thoughts were that he had done something very wrong and that Kramer was calling to reprimand him.

"Jesus, Perry, I just got a call from some bastard from Switzerland who said that he wants to meet me in London, of all places, to discuss taking over the company."

"What?" said Owen, simultaneously relieved and surprised.

"Look, the minute you get to work I want you to get a line on this guy. Have you got a pencil. His name is LeFevre and he has a bank in Geneva. He said he got my number from Geroge Hendricks at Hillman Flax. I want to know every last detail about that bastard.

Owen had never heard his boss so mad, so out of control. "Did he say if he was the company that has been accumulating all the stock."

"Yeah, yeah, they're the guys. Under the name

Monblank. Through a dinky broker in New York."

"Matthew Allyn & Co?"

"You know them?"

"I've seen their name on all the Monblank purchases."

"Right. Get a line on them too. I want to know everything about this son of a bitch, including which hand he uses to wipe himself."

"Yes sir." Owen was becoming stunned.

"Oh. And have the legal department waiting for me in my office when I arrive. I'll be in at nine. And cancel whatever you were doing for this weekend. You'll be coming to London with me. These guys are not just going to walk over us so easily."

Before Owen could respond, Kramer hung up the phone.

Owen changed out of his running clothes and went straight to the office. He immediately called Jon Smathers at Hillman, who, true to form, had already been at work for several hours.

"Jon, who is George Hendricks?"

"The partner who handles most of our European clients. Why?"

"Does the name LeFevre mean anything to you?"

Smathers instantly sat up straight. "Yes, I know of them. They are an important private banking firm in Geneva. We've done business with them for several years," he responded, trying to act casual.

"Well, would you have George Hendricks call me right away. I would like to know a little more about the firm."

"Certainly. Is there any way in which I can directly be of assistance?"

"No. Not really. I'm more interested in this LeFevre character. Wait, on second thought you can. Could you get me a line on this Matthew Allyn & Co.?"

"Who?" asked Smathers, sincerely. Big firms took little notice of their smaller competition. Owen spelled the name.

"You're not thinking of using them. They can't be up to our standard."

"We're not. No. But apparently LeFevre thought they were okay."

"Really. Well, I'll look into it for you."

"Thanks. Bye."

Smathers first called to Nick Bianco in the trading room. Fun before business, thought Smathers, who only applied that rule when it came to his own money.

"Nick. How's it going?"

"Just terrific. What's up?" Nick now welcomed calls from Smathers because he was sure that there would be some tipoff about the stock.

"Where's USOCO today?"

"$46 1/4, up 1/8. Why?"

"Oh, just curious. How are the August options doing?"

Nick checked the quotron machine. "$3." Smathers had already tripled his money. "Thinking of selling some?" asked Nick, somewhat deviously.

"Uh, what, no, I don't own any," he answered, realizing he almost gave it away. "Anyway, looks like a better time to buy than to sell," he added, trying to shift attention away from his near admission.

Nick heard all he needed to know. "Yeah, I guess," he responded, a master of the non-committal game. "Well, if there's nothing else, I'll get back to work."

The two hung up. Nick turned to the sales assistant and gave an order. "Buy another 100,000 shares of USOCO. No. Make it 200,000 shares." Nick could feel his heart pumping. This is the game he loved the most.

Smathers called Hendricks and relayed the message. Smathers realized that Hendricks now had been approached by LeFevre to get all the information he could about Kramer, and by Kramer to get all the information on LeFevre. Clearly, something was brewing. But Hendricks, unlike Smathers, was an old hand in this business. He had long since learned that playing tips or using inside information was a quick way to lose respect of your cusomters, the firm, and ultimately the SEC, who liked to exhibit their annoyance with fines, or even jail. Hendricks, for all his salesman bravado, knew how to keep his counsel.

"Andre LeFevre," he told Owen, "is a man of considerable charm, intelligence, sophistication, and

145

knowledge of financial affairs. His bank has been in business for nearly 100 years, and he has been the head of it for five years, having taken it over from his father. They have been a client of ours since the end of the war, and we naturally recommend doing business with them, if that is what you have in mind."

"What about the make-up of their clientele?" asked Owen.

"Very wealthy individuals, from all over the world."

"Would that include Arabs?"

"I don't know of any specifically, but I don't see why not. LeFevre & Cie. has an excellent reputation."

Not to us he doesn't, thought Owen, but out loud thanked Hendricks for his assistance. Owen was not encouraged by the reports.

Smathers called Owen back to give him whatever information he could scrounge upon Matthew Allyn & Co. It was limited to Matt and Whitey's background on the floor, but it was adequate to give Owen an idea of the types of individuals who ran that company. Owen then put in a call to that company. Matt picked up the phone.

"Hello. I would like to speak to either Matthew Allyn or Ted Whitehill."

"This is Matthew Allyn. Can I help you?"

"Yes. This is Owen Perry. I'm assistant to the CEO, Herbert Kramer, of the United States Oil Company and I would like to ask you a question or two."

Matt shifted uneasily in his chair. Owen's formal tone

had slightly intimidated him -- as if the caller had been from the FBI instead of USOCO.

"Yes. Certainly."

"Do you have a client by the name of LeFevre & Cie.?"

"Why do you want to know?" Matt, of course, had realized the meaning of the connection, but did not want to answer immediately. He recalled once having given out the name of a client to a governor on the floor of the Exchange during a dispute. The client ultimately heard about it from the governor and because of the disregard for the confidentiality, never did business with Matt again. Matt had learned his lesson.

"Because they named you as their broker -- and we do have you on record as having bought a large number of USOCO shares on behalf of a client. We want to know if LeFevre is that client."

Matt responded slowly. "I'm sorry, I'm really not at liberty to say."

"Very well," said Owen, clearly annoyed, "and thank you for your time."

Ten minutes later the phone rang again. Matt picked up with his usual greeting.

"Listen," said a gruff, clearly agitated voice. "This is Kramer from USOCO. All we want you to do is confirm what LeFevre has already told us. Have you bought more than 3% of our company on their behalf using the street name Monblank."

Matt thought slowly. Holy shit, there must be a takeover deal pending. Why else would LeFevre have called USOCO

147

directly and made that statement. Matt felt very uneasy. Clearly USOCO was not thrilled, and Matt did not wish to see himself in the middle.

"Um, well, I would like to be of help to you, but I prefer not to answer that question. Perhaps I can answer that later, after I speak to my, eh, lawyer," Matt almost said LeFevre instead of lawyer, but that would have given the game away.

"Okay, you speak to him, and you call us. We'll be waiting." Kramer hung up the phone with a bang.

Matt put in a phone call to LeFevre's office. Christine answered the phone.

"Christine," Matt said, "I would love to talk to you, but this is a business call to Andre."

"He is not here right now. I don't expect him back untill tomorrow morning." Christine answered formally. Then her voice lowered. "Oh Matt, I am so glad to talk to you. I have been so upset. I was going to call you tonight. I think there is something terrible going on here. But I can't talk now. Please wait for my call. Will you be home?"

Matt looked at his calandar. He had a cocktail party at 5. "Yes, certainly. I'll be in my apartment by 7 o'clock for sure. Is that too late for you.?"

"No, no. I'll call then. I'm sure I'll be awake." She quietly hung up the phone.

Matt felt very alarmed. He decided to cancel the cocktail party and call her earlier.

Smathers had considered the situation all day. He had $30,000 invested in options, which already were worth

$100,000. He mentally patted himself on the back for his ingenuity. He could cash in the $100,000, or he could go for even more. He considered the likely turn of events. If there was a takeover, the stock would surely go above $50, making his options worth even more. Even if only a rumor started, the price of the stock was sure to rise. Smathers went down to a phone booth in the lobby.

"Betsy. Hi. Look, take the remaining $10,000 we have and buy another 30 contracts of August USOCO options. That should run slightly over $9,000 plus commission. Yeah, I know that it's alot of USOCO, but have I been wrong so far. Be a good girl, and with the money, who knows what we'll do. Okay. Talk to you later. Bye."

CHAPTER THIRTY TWO

At four o'clock that afternoon, Matt called Christine from his private office. He knew by then that she would be at home and free to talk.

"Christine. What's the matter? What is going on?"

"Oh, Matt. I don't know. I know, I mean I think I'm sure now that Raoul Hengler must be stealing money from the company."

"How do you know that?"

Christine explained how she managed to get the files from Raoul's office. "But" she added, "there is no reason for him to keep a duplicate set of books unless he were embezzling. And he could do it. You see, he is the one that structures the entries into the computer. And he has a terminal to make corrections. In fact, he set up the system, so he knows all about it. He could do it very easily."

"Christine, you just must be mistaken. Not that I doubt that Raoul could easily steal money, if he wanted to, but it just doesn't make any sense. There's no real motive. Besides, not one customer has ever complained, have they?"

"No." Christine had to agree. "But they might never know. Most of them give full discretion to the bank to manage their money affairs, and never really look at their statements. So you see, that has no bearing on the matter."

"Okay. If you feel something is wrong, why don't you tell Andre LeFevre."

"That's just it. Oh, Matt. I think Mr. LeFevre is doing it with Raoul." She repeated word for word the conversation she overheard. "You see, it all ties in -- Raoul is keeping a different set of books and Andre knows all about it." Then Matt heard Christine's muffled sobs. She was clearly emotionally overwrought.

"Christine, Christine. That conversation proves nothing. Nothing at all. I think it's your imagination working overtime. Perhaps on both counts. After all, you spent a lot of money and did a lot of work to get those files -- you would like him to be guilty so that you can justify your effort."

He could hear Christine quiet down."Now, what I suggest is the following. First, take tomorrow off. Completely relax. Review all the information you have just accumulated and make certain of your conclusions. Then if you think that you are still right, go in to see Andre on the following day."

"Mr. LeFevre will be out of town the following day. He is going to London. I should do it tomorrow.

"No. Wait until after the weekend. This way you can be even more sure. And nothing will change overnight anyway."

"Oh, I wish you were here. I am so confused."

"Look. I'm planning my regular trip to Europe right now. If all my appointments work out, I will be there in two weeks. I'll try to get to Geneva first, but I may have to go to Dusseldorf for the weekend and then on to Switzerland. Why don't you wait for two weeks, then I can review the material with you. Maybe I can make better sense of it."

"Yes. Good. Okay. I'll wait. Yes. I would like a, well, second opinion. Oh, Matt, I wish it were sooner."

"It'll be quick enough. Now drink a cognac and get some sleep. I'll call you tomorrow."

"*Au'voir*," said Christine, considerably more relaxed.

"*Au'voir*," responded Matt. I love you, he added, in his head.

After speaking to Christine, he picked up the direct wire phone to call down to Whitey on the floor. He put it down again and thought for a second. Christine had to be wrong. If Raoul was embezzling money from the bank, surely it would have been noticed by now by someone else. He has been paying all of trades exactly on time -- someone would have picked up on a discrepancy if there had been a shortfall.

No, he thought. No use bothering Whitey with this now. Besides, he wouldn't believe that Christine could have simply tumbled on a bank fraud just like that. Besides, the last thing Whitey would want to hear is that there is a problem in the LeFevre account. Not when they were finally getting somewhere.

Matt sighed. It was just too fantastic to believe. She's just looking for a little excitement, he decided. He went back out of the office back to his trading desk.

"Where's USOCO now?" he asked. One of the assistants called out the quote. But his mind was so distracted, he didn't hear the answer.

CHAPTER THIRTY THREE

Kramer knocked on the door of suite #245 at the Connaught Hotel early Saturday morning. With him were Owen Perry and one of USOCO's house counsels, Lyle Steven. Andre LeFevre opened the door and escorted the trio in. Inside the room was Raoul Hengler. The three from the USOCO team sat to the left of the fireplace which dominated the living suite, the LeFevre duo sat to the right. There was a decided sense of confrontation in the air.

After introductions, LeFevre offered coffee and sweetrolls that had already been laid out by room service. Kramer declined. He knew he was on the weaker side in the negotiation play -- he was attending the meeting at LeFevre's bidding, at LeFevre's choice of location, to hear LeFevre's statement, at an hour which guaranteed that Kramer would be suffering from jet lag. He believed he was dealing with a professional. He did not want to be further obligated by accepting LeFevre's hospitality.

"No, thank you. In fact, we would appreciate your coming to the point. We are ready to hear what you have to say."

"Good. As you know my firm represents many wealthy

investors. Some of them are from the Middle East. One in particular is interested in your company. You see this individual is active in oil in his own country, and he has always been favorably impressed by your company.

He asked me to begin to accumulate some shares for him, naturally without any fanfare, which, of course, I have been more than pleased to do. Currently we have more than 3% of your stock, which cost my investor approximately $1 billion. Although this seems like a large amount of money, to my investor it is merely a small portion of his fortune, and he is quite willing to acquire more. Indeed, he would like to own a majority of your company."

Kramer's face hardened at this comment -- it was entirely expected, but not the least bit more welcome. Andre continued:

"Since the price of USOCO stock has continued to rise, based on rumors that are always prevalent in the market, my client feels that he cannot continue to buy more shares without further inflating their price past what he considers a reasonable amount. He is therefore willing to make a deal. He would like you and your Board of Director's blessing on our offer to put an offer to your stockholders to buy their shares at approximately $55 a share, or $10 over the current asking price."

Kramer broke in. "Who is this guy? What is his name?"

"Unfortunately I am not at liberty to tell you this at this time. My client knows that when he has accummulatd 5% of your company's stock he must make himself known to the company and the SEC as a shareholder. But until that time, he wishes to remain anonymous."

"Well, if he doesn't tell us his name, how can I put forth a real offer to the Board."

"Oh, I understand your American boards of directors. They already know if they wish to sell the company and at what price. Most often it is merely a matter of money. So the question to begin is whether the $55 offer is acceptable."

"No, it isn't acceptable. I'm not even going to suggest it."

"That is too bad. Beacuse you see, my client has carefully taken this possibility into consideration. You see, if there is a friendly takeover, then he would be willing to buy at $55 per share, and to offer the current management one year employment contracts.

"If your Board does not agree to such a thing, my client will take this matter directly to the stockholders. He realizes that stockholders often have to be swayed in their thinking, but he is willing to go as high as $75 dollars a share to gain a majority ownership. The company's stock has not been that high since 1973. He believes that even those who might be opposed to foreign ownership might see certain benefits to giving up their rights. My client expects that he could easily attract 50% of the shareholders in that fashion."

"And the management?"

"Ah, my client could guarantee nothing. After all, during these kinds of takeovers unkind words are occasionally said. It would be very difficult to work for someone whom you opposed so vehemently before."

"Well, we have to know who this guy is before I can say anything."

"All I can tell you right now is that he is from one of the Gulf Emirates. And a man of excellent reputation, of course."

Kramer scowled. Excellent reputation. Shit. A goddam

sandkicker. Probably smells like one of his camels.
Goddamn son-of-a-bitch.

"I can tell you now the answer is no. I'm not even going
to make a formal proposal to the Board. The company is not
for sale. Period. I'm just goddam sorry you had me come all
the way here to have to say this. But this is the worst idea I
have heard in my whole career."

Andre feigned remorse. "I am so sorry to hear you
speak in this fashion. You see I was so sure that you would
be interested in our offer that I made reservations for dinner
tonight in the grill downstairs, during which my assistant
would give you all the refinements on the proposal necessary
for your lawyers."

Kramer stood up. He had had his fill of this arrogant,
pompous man who presumes that USOCO would grab at any
bone tossed their way.

"I'll be giving something to my lawyers, all right.
Because we will be fighting you tooth and nail on this. So,
since it is unlikely that we can have further meaningful words
to say to each other, I would like to bid you good day."
Kramer and his entourage walked out.

As soon as they closed the door behind them, Andre
picked up the phone and put in a call to The London
Economic Times. He asked to speak to Robert Grantner,
one of the journalists.

"Hello, Bob. How are you? Listen, I'm in London.
Can we meet for lunch? Yes. Excellent. I'm hearing lots of
rumors these days and I always like to catch up on the truth.
Rumors on who? USOCO, for instance. Apparently, a bid
has been made. You haven't heard. Well, I'll fill you in on
what I've heard at lunch. Come here to the Connaught, I'll
make a reservation. One o'clock. Fine. See you then."

Andre then dialed room service. "Send up a bottle of Moet Chandon, Brut, please." He looked at Raoul. He was smiling broadly. "To celebrate a job well done," added Lefevre.

CHAPTER THIRTY FOUR

The next Tuesday, as Jack McGrory entered his stretch Seville limousine in front of his apartment at 75th and Park, his chauffeur handed him the day's Wall Street Journal. Shifting his overweight and stiff body in an effort to get comfortable, Jack quickly turned to the inside back page to check out the "Heard on the Street" column. It covered street rumors and was the Journal's most influential column -- influential, that is, from the point of view of affecting the price of whatever stock or industry group was analyzed in the piece. Jack knew that if any of the stocks in which he made a market was involved, the action that day would be intense and furious.

"Mary, Mother of God," exclaimed Jack. "Get a load of this fucking article."

USOCO PRICE RISE ATTRIBUTED TO REPORTED
TAKEOVER INTEREST BY ARAB INVESTORS --
STOCK ANALYSTS SKEPTICAL

Unconfirmed reports circulated that Arab investors will make a bid for fifty percent of USOCO's shares at $75 per *share. Close checks with Wall Street sources revealed an unusual absence of information among take-over experts concerning potential suitors.*

In New York Stock Exchange trading yesterday, USOCO stock closed at 47 1/4, up 1 1/8 on heavy volume of 1,600,000 shares.

A spokesman for USOCO, Owen Perry, assistant to the CEO, Herbert Kramer, said the company didn't know of any reason for the stock's activity. In response to a Big Board inquiry, Mr. Kramer said, "There is nothing to substantiate the rumors regarding a possible takeover of the company."

Merger activity in the oil industry has surged in recent years, primarily because it's become easier to acquire reserves than to discover them.

Some analysts have speculated that USOCO could become a takeover target, because of its relatively low stock price and strong reserves. But they also point out that with 750 million shares outstanding a takeover of this magnitude could be prohibitively expensive.

The article continued to chronicle USOCO's price rise over the past six months and the unusually heavy trading in the stock. Jack's eyebrows were further raised when towards the end of the piece the brokerage firm of Matthew Allyn & Co. was mentioned as the broker for the unnamed purchaser.

"Well, I'll be a son of a bitch", wheezed Jack, as he pulled out another of his forbidden Marlboro cigarettes. "Whitey's got himself a tiger by the tail".

Jack dreaded the beginning of the trading day, only two hours hence. The buyers were going to rip his balls off!

CHAPTER THIRTY FIVE

The days that followed the printing of the article were tumultuous. The stock, as Jack anticipated, was overwhelmed with buyers. Its price rose three points on that day, and another five points the following day, bringing the price of the stock to $55. Jack had taken a whopping loss on those two days' trading alone, over $3 million disappeared from his capital, bringing his total loss to $15 million. When he hit $20 million in losses, his firm would have to call it quits. He was now putting away up to a pack a day -- smoked mostly at night because no smoking was allowed on the floor. Were it not for that restriction it would have been closer to three packs.

Matt was arriving even earlier at the office. If any messages came through from Europe, he wanted to be able to respond immediately. On Friday, Whitey also showed at an unusually early hour -- carrying in a hard roll and milk for breakfast, as if he were anticipating the onslaught of an ulcer attack.

"Hey," said Matt. "You're early."

"Yeah. I'm not sleeping well."

"That's because you're sleeping alone."

"Ha, ha. No, it's this fucking USOCO business. One minute I think I know what's going on, the next minute I'm like in fantasyland."

"Yeah. I know," said Matt, half heartedly. Matt had still not said anything to Whitey about Christine's adventures. No use creating anxiety. "The pieces all fit together in the puzzle, but it doesn't make a picture," he added.

"Well, if you look at it from one angle, LeFevre has managed to accumulate enough shares of a stock for some Arab to make any takeover a real possiblity."

"Yeah, but who leaked that story? And why? Why doesn't Andre just continue on his buying spree till he hits more than 5%, and then announce his intentions. All the leak of that story does is jack up the price."

"Yeah, and jack Jack around." Whitey laughed at his joke, but Matt didn't notice.

"Unless, oh, shit."

"What, what?" Whitey prompted. Matt hesitated -- he still wasn't ready to discuss Christine's findings.

"Unless there is no Arab. Unless LeFevre can't wait till 5% of the shares are bought because then he would have to lay down his cards. Unless this is one big scam."

"But for what purpose? Granted they got the price of the stock up, but they're in too deep to just start selling off the shares. It would knock the price down to the levels they bought them at, making it nothing more than an exercise in futility."

Whitey and Matt looked at each other. Suddenly the picture came into focus for both of them.

"Jesus. They're planning on greenmail. They want USOCO to buy them off at a high price. They're hoping that USOCO will be so afraid that an Arab might be running their company that they would rather pay any price to buy the shares back."

"Holy fuck. We've been such assholes. We should have seen this one coming five months ago. We were so busy staring at the $4,000 bill they gave us everyday that we couldn't see past our asses."

"So Andre leaked that story."

"But why to the London Economic Times?"

Matt remembered Christine saying that LeFevre was in London over the weekend. " Because he was in London then. Because, knowing Andre, he probably has a friend on the newspaper. Because he has every move of the game down tight, and we, like the newspaper guys, are just his patsies."

Whitey fell silent. "Yeah, but so far he has paid us a million five in commissions for our efforts. And when he sells, there will be even more commissions. And since we did nothing wrong, nothing at all, I'd say we're pretty rich patsies."

Matt smiled. Whitey was right. Matthew Allyn & Company did all right. And did nothing wrong. They were rich -- and were going to become richer. Without any effort. So why the worry?

The phone rang.

"May I speak to Matthew Allyn, please," the caller asked.

"Speaking."

"This is John Swerman from the Wall Street Journal. Would you care to comment on the USOCO purchases being made by LeFevre. Is there a real takeover pending? Do you know who the Arab is?"

"Eh." Matt thought for a moment. If he commented, then his firm's name would be in the paper -- a rare privilege for a smaller brokerage firm. But what was there to say. He certainly couldn't answer the questions in the affirmative, and answering in the negative could be disasterous.

"Eh, I'm really not at liberty to say anything."

"Well, what about LeFevre. Have they bought as many shares as are rumored?"

"Well, eh, they did buy a lot."

"But as much as 5%. That's more than a lot. That's $2 billion dollars worth, by my estimation."

Damn, these guys knew how to wrangle out an answer. "Well, eh, they own some."

"How much is some? Is there a takeover going on?"

"I can't answer that right now."

"Come on. You've haven't even given me enough to print. I need something to say."

Matt fell silent. He could see his possiblity of a moment of fame fleeting away. "What can I tell you?" he finally said. "There's nothing more I can add."

"Well. If you think of anything, call me." The journalist left the number for his direct line. Matt made a note of it. Never hurt to have a friend in the press.

The phone rang again. Shit, thought Matt, these journalists are early risers.

But it wasn't the press -- it was Horst, calling from Dusseldorf.

"Horst, *wie geht's*."

"Ganz gut. Are you coming to stay with me next weekend?"

Matt would rather have been in Geneva. "Why, is anything particularly special going on."

"Yes, it should be a big weekend. There's a fox hunt at the club and I invited several of my banking friends. Lars and I are going to ride."

"Lars. Lars who?"

"My horse," snapped Horst.

"Right. Of course. But what other bankers are going to be there. Andre?"

"No. He's apparently tied up with this USOCO affair. He's really doing big things."

"Right." Matt had to agree there. He was sorry that he had planned his trip for this time period. Everything would probably pop while he was away. But he had already committed to several appointments, and he didn't want to back off. Besides, this hunt club affair seemed like another opportunity to meet more people.

"Well, do we see you next Saturday? That's February the 15th."

"I'd be delighted." Christine will just have to wait a few more days.

"Terrific. My secretary will send you the details."

After the conversation, Whitey asked Matt, "Didn't Horst buy shares of USOCO as well."

Matt pulled Horst's name up on the computer screen.

"Yeah. 50,000 shares at $35 in October, and another 100,000 shares at $45 in January."

"Sounds like he got a tip from Andre."

"Must have. Well, as I always say, better lucky than smart."

CHAPTER THIRTY SIX

Max Adler was on the phone with Marty Fishbein, the nervous investor in the syndicate.

"Marty, things are great. The news is terrific. How can you want to pull out now -- this stock is good to $65 at least."

"Max. You're smart. There's no doubt about it, you're smart. When I wanted to pull out last time, you convinced me to stay in. And as a result I now am $300,000 richer -- which is not exactly a tragedy. But it's getting to my gut. You know what I mean. I can't sleep from worry. What if this thing explodes. I got a lot of money tied up in it."

"You want out. Is that what you're saying? There's a big takeover going on in the stock and you want out."

"Max, don't be hard on me. I'm just a little tailor with a few pennies. I'm not a genius like you. These takeovers have a way of falling through. I only want to sleep at night."

"Okay, Marty. I'm here to take care of my customers. But I'm telling you, this is going to be like taking candy from a baby. It's the only game in the market, and buyers are out there ready to play. But if you want to take your money early, I'm not stopping you. We'll sell out your portion."

"Ah, Max. Stop making me feel like such a schmuck. I'm only doing this for my health."

"Don't worry Marty. We'll get you out by this afternoon. Then you can use those *schmata* you make as crying towels later."

"Thanks. I'm sorry, Max. I just wasn't cut out for the big time."

After Max hung up the phone, he called Jimbo on the phone. "Sell out 12,000 shares of USOCO and send the proceeds to Marty Fishbein." Max then opened his deskdrawer and took out the list of names he kept there. Very deliberately, he drew a thick line through Marty Fishbein's name. Risk arbitrage was not a game for little minds, he thought.

At about the same time, Betsy was on the phone to Smathers.

"You shouldn't be calling me in the office," he said to her crossly.

"I'm sorry. But the broker called. About those, uh, things. He thinks you should sell. Oh, honey, you've, we've already made a lot of money. Can't we just take it and run."

"Betsy," Smathers said as sternly as he could in a whisper. "Those 'things' have a way to go yet. We're on to a real winner, so don't give it up so quickly."

"But, Jon, some of that money is mine and I don't want to lose it. The broker said that anything could happen. Can't we at least sell some of it?"

"I'll tell you when to sell. I know what's going on -- not that jackass in Boston. So don't listen to him, listen to me."

"Can't we just sell some of it."

Smathers was becoming even more impatient. "No," he shouted loud enough for those outside his office to hear. He could hear Betsy whimper.

"Bets, I'm sorry. I didn't mean to shout. Look, just be patient. If everything works out, we will have a big enough nest egg to get married. How about that."

It worked -- Betsy's mind was on to the marriage. "Really. You mean it? Okay, Jon. I'll wait for your instructions."

Jon hung up the phone. He was wondering how he would get out of making good on his promise to marry when he cashed in on the options.

On the other side of the office building, Nick was having a conversation with his boss, Hillman Flax's President.

"I see we have a very large position in USOCO. Isn't that a little treacherous?"

"Not as I see it. I think the market is just really getting a second wind. With luck we will be able to squeeze quite a few more dollars out of it."

"With luck. I really don't want to bet so much of the firm's money up on lucky chances. I think we should slim down our position. We already have taken quite a bit out of the stock. Why push it?"

"But the stock market is still going sideways. This is the only stock that shows any real promise. We have to place on bets here, because there is nothing else."

"If you are such a hot trader, you would be able to find something else."

Nick bristled at that remark. Such things were easier to say than to do.

"Look, I feel very confident about this stock. I'm sure that we can pull more out it. I don't want to sell out now."

"Is that your decision?"

"Yes," said Nick sharply, wanting to sound as confident as possible.

"Then okay. But if it goes against you, as they say, your ass will be grass."

Don't I know it, thought Nick. "Don't worry, it won't. I can move fast if and when things turn." I hope, he added mentally.

On the following Tuesday, Herbert Kramer was addressing a special meeting of the Board of Directors of USOCO in Houston.

"As you probably have all read, there are a considerable

number of rumors going on about a possible raid on our stock. I don't know who started them, but I can guess. In any case that is not relevant. What is relevant is the substance of that takeover offer.

"Last week in London, Andre LeFevre of LeFevre & Cie. gave our company, that is, me personally, a verbal offer of $55 per share to purchase all the outstanding shares of USOCO. The real buyer's identity is not known, but we were told that he is an Arab.

"If we did not accept their offer of $55 per share for a friendly takeover, LeFevre indicated that the Arab would be willing to go to $75 for a tender offer to the public.

"I told them to go to hell."

The members of the Board murmered. "Without asking us first," said one of them.

"Do you want your comapny run by some asshole Arab?" aked Kramer, showing visible signs of agitation. The members silently shook their heads.

"Then what was the point of pursuing it?"

"But is it a serious threat? Could he actually afford to make a tender offer for the whole company?"

"Gentlemen, in the interim I have been looking into this matter. While we did not make much headway on the identity of the Arab, we have no reason to believe that it is not a valid attempt to buy our company. Accordingly, I would like to propose that we buy him out."

"But that's greenmail."

"I know. But we have no choice. We can't afford to let

this get any further. I'm not in the mood for a proxy battle, and we can probably buy the shares for $55, the current market price. If the price of the shares holds on the market, it won't be too costly."

The Chairman of the Board stood up.

"Mr. Kramer, before we make this decision we would like to discuss this among ourselves. We will call you tomorrow with our conclusion. If we do decide to buy out the position of LeFevre, we will contact you by tomorrow, so that you can start immediate action. I agree that we should not let the price of the stock on the market get to far out of hand before we act."

Kramer walked out of the meeting feeling confident that they would vote as he proposed. He was pleased that he was working with a understanding Board. He was sure they would see his point of view. He tried to imagine Arabs sitting around that table instead of Americans. Aaagh. He wouldn't have been able to tolerate a bunch of Jew-killing Arabs pushing him around.

CHAPTER THIRTY SEVEN

That afternoon Matt put through a call to Christine, who was just getting ready for bed.

"Christine, how are you? How are you holding up?"

"I am all right now, Matt. I'm doing more thinking about what I saw. Perhaps things are not as terrible as I make them seem. I'm probably overdramatizing."

Matt felt relieved. "Well, I'm not underestimating you. I think under that feminine exterior you are one very sharp cookie."

"Cookie?"

"Just an expression -- it means you are smart?"

Christine laughed a little, which Matt was pleased to hear. He missed her usual perkiness.

"Listen, I'm sorry to say that I won't be able to see you until Sunday evening.I have to be in Dusseldorf on Saturday. To watch a fox hunt of all things."

"Yes, I bet I know with who. Horst Meyer at his hunt club, right?"

"Yes. How did you know?"

"Mr. Lefevre was also invited, but I had to decline for him. He has some big matter he is involved with."

"That's the USOCO deal. Surely you know what's going on?"

"Not really. Just a lot more meetings than usual with Raoul."

Matt thought for a minute. "Christine, I have a question for you. Have you been putting any calls through to the Middle East?"

"No, why? You keep asking about Arab customers."

Matt was not surprised at the answer. "I have another quick question -- does Andre have any friends among the financial journalists in London?"

"Well, there's Robert Grantner. He works for the Economic Times. Why, do you want his number?"

"No, but let me give you one -- where I'll be staying in Germany. I'll be at the Breidenbacher Hof, that's 86-01 in Dusseldorf. Call me if you find anything. I should be there early Saturday morning."

"Okay. But I won't call unless there is a problem."

"Call anytime." Matt meant it. "Call me at the hunt club if you want. I'll be there at about 11 o'clock."

"Shall I call there and make it sound like an important message is awaiting you. Would that impress the other guests?"

Matt laughed -- yes, it probably would. "Christine, I can't wait to see you. I'll be at the Hotel du Rhone by six at the latest. I call you as soon as I arrive."

"D'accord. Au'voir."

"Au'voir. Je t'aime."

After a few minutes, Matt returned his thoughts to business matters. He now was certain that there were no Arabs involved, that it was only a greenmail ploy. Matt considered his own firm's position. Outside of buying the shares for LeFevre, they had no direct hand in the takeover bid. Therefore, they could never be accused of any misrepresentation -- which LeFevre was certainly open to -- if, that is, anyone ever found him out.

But who was to find him out. With that story he leaked he made everything sound very credible. He probably had Kramer so scared of being taken over by Arabs that Kramer would rather pay than even speak to one of them. Matt put Andre up several notches in his estimation of his intelligence, but down as many on the integrity score. Andre was someone decidedly to be wary of.

CHAPTER THIRTY EIGHT

At four o'clock on Friday afternoon, Andre read a telex that he had just received over the bank's main machine.

To Andre LeFevre.

We are hereby placing a bid for the entire holding of your client(s) of United States Oil Company common stock at the price of $65 per share. This offer is final and must be accepted and tendered no later than Tuesday, February 18, at 12:01PM Houston time. If a negative response or no response is made by that time, we will assume that your client(s) will continue in there bid for a takeover of USOCO. This is to inform you on behalf of the Board of Directors and the management of USOCO that we intend to fight any attempt by a foreigner to gain control of a company that is vital to the interests of the United States, and we will use all legal means to do so.

Signed, H. Kramer.

Not necessary, thought Andre, we are delighted to accept your bid for $65. Andre picked up the private wire to Raoul.

"Raoul, I want you to take the rest of the day off."

Such an odd demand to make of a workaholic. "Why. Am I doing something wrong?"

"*Au contraire.* You have done everything right. We just received a telex from USOCO."

"And?"

"And they fell for it. To the tune of $65 per share"

Raoul did some quick figuring -- it worked out to a profit of $500 million. Raoul let out a whoop. The trading room personnel all turned to look -- their dour faced boss rarely exhibited positive emotions.

"When?" he finally calmed down enough to ask.

"On Tuesday. Actually, I'm surprised at that. Why not Monday?"

"Oh, I know why. Because Monday is Washington's Birthday in the U.S. Everything is closed."

"Oh, no matter. I can wait the extra day."

"But what if Kramer decides by Monday to call the whole deal off."

"Don't worry. I have a little plan that will keep the pressure on him."

"I'll bet it involves the press."

"Right. You are very smart -- but I always knew that."

"In that case I deserve the day off."

"And you shall have it. And, this evening I am going to buy you the best meal in Geneva. Come to my office as soon as you have finished up there. You'll have to contact Matthew Allyn and tell them to have the shares ready on Tuesday for tendering to USOCO. I'll give them the exact location later."

Thank God, thought Raoul, as he went into his closet to send that telex off to Matt. Thank God at last.

Andre called Christine into his office. "Please take a dictation to be sent by telex:

"To H. Kramer:

"My client regrets that his attempt to share in the glory of your company was not well received, but he understands that there may be excellent reasons for your wishing the company not to be foreign dominated. Accordingly, he accepts your offer of $65 dollars a share. The shares will be available for tendering on Tuesday, as you requested. I will contact you by phone Tuesday morning in your office to confirm details. Signed, A. LeFevre"

After Christine finished the dictation, she started to leave the office. She had been avoiding any eye contact with Andre since she overheard the discussion. She doubted if he even noticed.

"By the way, I'll be leaving the office shortly. Would you be certain to get that telex out by this evening. And would you make reservations for two at Le Bearn at 8PM."

"Certainly. Then you and Mrs. LeFevre will be going off to Gstaad later?"

178

"No, we will probably leave tomorrow. This evening is my treat to Raoul Hengler." Christine looked at him directly. "For all the hard work he has put in lately," Andre added, smiling.

"Of course," she said, wondering if he noticed the look of surprise on her face.

After Christine left the room, Andre picked up the phone and dialed a London number. "Bob," said Andre "I think I have something more dramatic for you than the last story you published in the Economic Times."

A few minutes later, Raoul came to Andre's office. Christine could see Raoul reading a telex closely, then Andre folding it and putting it in his coat pocket. After that the two left for the evening. They were in a high mood, particularly Raoul, who even gave Christine a quick smile.

CHAPTER THIRTY NINE

Christine finished her day's work, including the special telex. The other employees left at five, leaving Christine alone in the office again. She knew that Hengler would definitely be tied up for the evening, but she didn't see what use it would be to rifle through his files once more. She had seen at least twenty of the files already, and they all were of the same type. She decided to leave the office as well. Matt would be there on Sunday, only two days away. Perhaps he could give her a little more peace of mind.

She made a light supper for herself at her apartment and opened a bottle of dole. Two glasses into the wine she began to feel more relaxed. She started reading a book, but her mind couldn't stick to the pages. By eight o'oclock she started to get restless. She knew that Andre and Raoul would be just settling down to the beginning of meal that should last at least two hours. She closed her book, got dressed and went back to the bank.

The guard was surprised to see her.

"Oh, Herr Ringgli. Would you believe that I forgot to send out a most important letter. Monsieur LeFevre would be just furious if he knew that I did not get it out."

"Oh, my dear, you are working too hard."

"Not at all. It shouldn't take me more than an hour."

Christine went back down to Hengler's office. Not worrying about time, she felt more comfortable going through each of the files thoroughly. She still saw only headings referring to customers' accounts. There was nothing that suggested that the bank's own funds had been manipulated.

As she placed the cabinet's keys back in Raoul's desk, she saw a manila file that she had not noticed before. She pulled it out. In it were ledger pages again written by hand, which showed various dates and amounts. Hardly any headings were written, so there was no way to tie the numbers to anything else. Christine made some copies, but felt that she had not uncovered anything of real value.

She went back to her own desk to assemble the papers and leave. The evening's excursion was in vain after all. Then she remembered the telephone call she overheard in which Andre requested the 'final numbers' be sent to him. Maybe something was in Andre's office. She had never dared search it before -- until the other day she had trusted Andre implicitly.

Christine turned on the light to his office. The elegant French atmosphere made it imposing, almost untouchable -- a museum. The winter darkness made Christine feel even more like an interloper -- someplace she did not belong.

She went to Andre's Louis Quinze desk and sat at his chair. The drawers of the desk were not locked -- Andre must have forgotten in his rush to get out. Slowly, as if she expected a spring snake to jump out, she opened each of the drawers. Most contained papers she was already familiar with. A bottom drawer contained several empty Tobler chocalate bar wrappers -- Christine smirked -- it hadn't occurred to her that Andre might be a secret chocolate freak. None of the drawers revealed anything unusual.

181

She turned to the credenza. It was as high as the desk in a style similar to the rest of the room, but it was a recently made piece, designed on the interior to hold files and ledgers. Christine tugged at the top drawer. Locked. She checked in the desk for the key -- but none were there. She tugged at the bottom drawer. It opened. The two drawers must have an independent locking system. She slowly pulled it wide.

It was full of reports thrown in ramdomly, as if by someone who cleans off the desk in the evening by just sweeping one's hands across it. Some of the reports were hand written, some typed. Most contained information about past trading records, price comparisons, the summaries to commodity values, the values of gold, purchase dates. On each of the handwritten reports she recognized Raoul's script. She pulled some out for closer review.

It took more than a half hour of close study, but suddenly a picture was beginning to come into focus. Before her were the results of the bank's activities in various trading accounts over different periods of time. They were terrible. Losses predominated every sheet she looked at. She was stunned. She knew that Andre set the policy for the trading and according to these records he was a miserable failure. Why then did all of the customers rave of his success?

The truth was slowly dawning. Raoul was not embezzling funds, by himself -- it was Andre who was directing a massive cover-up of the bank's losses. Christine rummaged through all of the papers. Nothing conclusive was found -- just more reports of the losses. Somewhere there must be books which showed the bank's full accounts, both the real and the fraudulently adjusted ones. She tugged again at the credenza's top drawer. It would not give.

Suddenly the phone rang. Christine jumped. Was Andre calling to ask what she was doing there? What would she say? She would say that she forgot to send the telex? Would he believe her? Carefully she picked up the phone.

"Fraulein Evins. This is Herr Ringgli. Are you still working? I am beginning to worry about you."

"Oh, Herr Ringgli, it's you. I, uh, I am almost finished. You will see me in a moment."

Christine grabbed all the papers she could find and ran to the duplicator. After making copies, she returned the originals back to the drawer, closed up the office, threw on her overcoat and ran downstairs. She wished Herr Ringgli a good night, and took a taxi back to her apartment.

As soon as she entered she dialed Matt number at the office. It would be about 4:30 in the afternoon there. Jerry Stern, Matt's assistant answered.

"Gee, I'm sorry Christine, but Matt has already left for the airport."

Christine gasped. She would have to wait to reach him tomorrow. She knew she faced a completely sleepless night.

CHAPTER FORTY

Matt's flight, which was considerably emptier than the one last summer, nevertheless left two hours late due to a leaky valve in the wing. Instead of arriving at Dusseldorf at six in the morning, it arrived at eight. Matt considered the timing problem it was causing him. It would take a half hour to get to downtown Dusseldorf to the Breidenbacher, another half hour to wash and change, and another forty five minutes to get to the hunt club. That would leave about an hour to catch some sleep -- which, when added to the three cramped hours worth he got on the plane, would be just too little to make him feel rested. Matt envisioned himself looking like death warmed over while he was being introduced to a new round of German bankers. He decided to skip checking into the Breidenbach until that evening and to take a room at the Airport Hilton for the morning, which, because it was much closer to the club, would allow him an extra hour of shut eye.

As a result of this decision, he did not get any of the messages Christine had been leaving for him at the Breidenbach since six o'clock that morning.

Matt arrived at the club at 11:00 on the button, dressed in a blue blazer, a tan turtleneck sweater and gray flannel

184

slacks. Horst was already in the center of a group of his guests -- each one was dressed in more traditional German riding wear -- tweed hacking jackets with high green velvet collars -- except for Horst, who was wearing the red jacket associated with fox hunting. Matt was very conscious of being the outsider. In addition, the coversation was being held solely in German, which Matt handled more haltingly than French. He wondered how he was going to make a favorable enough impression to gain entrance to their private offices during the work week.

Horst introduced Matt all around and left to prepare for his ride. That would start at about 11:30, after which a hunt luncheon would be served. Matt learned that a real fox was no longer used. The beagles, who were not fed that morning, were given the scent of beef entrails, which they would "chase" over the planned course, and finally be allowed to eat at the finish. That softened Matt's feeling about the hunt, for he disdained unnecessary killing. Neverthless, he felt that it might be a long, uncomfortable . day for him.

Just as he was beginning to enter the conversation with slightly more ease, he heard his name being paged over a loudspeaker. "Herr Allyn, Herr Allyn, please come to the telephone for a call."

Hah, thought Matt, that's Christine. Coming to my rescue after all. In fact, it did have the effect Matt imagined. The others in the group kidded Matt aboutnot being able to get away from business, even in Germany. "Maybe it's your mother," said one, but even that old chestnut brought more favorable attention to him.

"Hello, Christine?"

"Yes, it's me."

"Well, I think it worked beautifully. Everyone is impressed."

"Oh, Matt. That's not why I called. I've been trying to reach you everywhere." Matt sensed the tremor in her voice.

"What is it?"

"It's Andre LeFevre. I now know what has been going on. Andre and Raoul -- they have been stealing from the firm. Together."

"Christine -- are you sure. Are you absolutely sure?"

"Yes. I mean no. I mean I have everything but the papers that show that the books were changed. But everything that I do have points to a, a, you know. You must come. You must see it for yourself."

"Why me. You should take it to the Swiss banking department if you think you are right."

"Yes, I want to. But I must be absolutely sure. It is a very grave offense here, you know. Everyone would go to jail. Oh, Matt. Please come."

"Okay. I will come right away. I'll catch the next plane out of here. Stay in your apartment until I arrive."

"Matt." Christine hesitated.

"Yes."

"I'm scared."

"Don't be. I'll be there as soon as I can."

"I can't help it. I keep thinking that someone knows

what I have been doing."

"Okay. I'll tell you what. Wait for me at the hotel --
that's the Hotel du Rhone -- with the papers. No one could
possibly find you there."

"Okay, I'll be in the lobby."

"Don't worry Christine. It's going to be all right."

Matt hung up the phone and started to look for Horst,
who he finally located outside the stable holding on to his
mount. The air was chilly, almost cold, and the horse was
blowing large breaths of mist from his nostrils.

"Horst, I must leave."

"Leave? But why?"

"I have to go to Geneva."

"So soon. Has it something to do with Andre? I know
you were working with him on the USOCO deal."

"It has something to do with Andre all right. But not the
USOCO deal. Horst, I think Andre might have been
embezzling funds." Matt regretted having said that, but then,
Horst was an old trusted friend.

Horst was turning pale. "You are joking me."

"No. But if so, I'll need to get to the head of the Central
Bank in Switzerland. I'll probably be there on Monday."

"You mean Hans Garweiler?"

Matt recognized the name of the leading Swiss banker.
"If that's who it is."

"But what about the USOCO takeover."

"There's no takeover, Horst. It's all a scam made up by Andre. That will fall through as well."

"And the value of the stock?"

Matt shrugged his shoulders. "What difference does it make. It'll be just another failed takeover story. Lots of stocks have been through that mill."

At first, Horst stared into space. The he began to shout. "You fucking bastards. All of you. You use us for your own purposes, and you don't care who gets hurt. *Schweine.*"

Matt started to back off. He had never seen Horst so mad. He could not imagine what was the basis of his anger. Other riders who were preparing for the hunt turned and stared. Horst was still shouting. Matt began to run. In the distance he could hear a hunting horn sound off to gather the hunters. The beagles, already restless from hunger, started to bark ever louder. By the time Matt reached the front of the club, he was shaking from fear.

He calmed down enough to ask the clerk behind the front desk to order a taxi to the airport. One would arrive in ten minutes. Matt debated going back into the club to the group of bankers. He looked inside and saw that they had all moved out to the corral area to watch the hunters take off. Some had arranged to follow the route in vans -- others would stay behind, passing the time at the bar. Matt moved towards them, walking past the tack house. He also was beginning to be frightened.

A thought struck him. He turned and entered the tack house.

He saw the old tackmaster standing near the window, watching the spectacle. What was his name? Something to do with circuses. Ringling? No, Matt suddenly remembered.

"Herr Barnum," he called out, "Horst Meyer has forgotten something and asked me if I would retrieve it from his tackbox. Would you open it quickly for me."

Herr Barnum nodded and moved quickly to open the box with his master key. He went back to watching the hunt, which was just at the point of beginning.

Matt saw what he wanted. Inside the box lay three guns -- a .22 caliber rifle, a shotgun, and a luger. Matt reached for the luger and slipped in into his pocket. This should calm our fears, he thought. He shouted thanks to Herr Barnum and left to get the cab.

He picked up his bags at the Hilton, slipped the luger in the luggage, grabbed a cab, and was able to catch a flight leaving only forty minutes later. Settling into his window seat on the jet, he took a deep breath and attempted to relax. All his physical functions, his heart beat, his pulse, seemed to be moving at double time, except for his mind, which seemed twice as slow. His thoughts were jumbled nonsense. As the plane took off he closed his eyes and tried rhythmic breathing to get a better control of his body.

Suddenly his eyes opened. "Jesus Christ," he said out loud, barely aware of the passenger sitting two seats away from him. Matt look out the window to hide his embarrassment -- not just from the remark but from what he had just realized.

Matthew Allyn, made the fool of again, he thought. What an ass. You should have put this one together a long time ago, kid. You had all the clues. It was just like the time you were hazed on the floor of the Exchange. If you had only looked up, you would have known it was a fraud. Now, if you had only stopped to think, you'd had seen the picture.

If there was no Arab investor, he had realized, then the money had to come from somewhere else to make all the payments for the stock. It had to have come from the bank's other funds, those that were placed in trust to purchase the customers' investment holdings. And since those investors did not know they were buying USOCO stock -- Christine had confirmed that -- Andre must have been raiding the funds in those accounts surreptitiously to gather that much money. All to pull off this caper. And he has come close to succeeding.

Why did it have to happen before the takeover was completed. It the whole deal went through, Matt's firm would make another $1 million for tendering the shares. That's at least another $500,000 each for Whitey and himself. Oh. God. Why does everything have to fall apart just as it was beginning to look good.

Matt drew a very deep breath. Maybe Christine is all wrong, he thought. Maybe it is just as LeFevre says -- an Arab deal. Please God, let her be mistaken. Please God, let this deal go through.

He thought of his comments to Horst. Hopefully Horst wouldn't say anything to anyone. At least not before Matt had a chance to talk to him again.

CHAPTER FORTY ONE

When the hunt concluded Horst returned to the club. He passed by his guests with a nod and went straight to the club's telephones. First he put in a call to Geneva, and getting no answer there, put in another one to Gstaad.

"Ah, Horst," answered Andre. "I was planning on calling you on Monday. To tell you the good news. You should now sell out your position in USOCO."

"If there is a Monday," said Horst sharply.

"What do you mean? Horst, are you feeling all right?"

"Did you embezzle funds from your own bank?"

Andre was silent for a second. "That's preposterous. Why do you even ask it?"

"Because Matt Allyn thinks so and he is ready to go to Garweiler to tell him."

"Where is he seeing Garweiler? Here? In Gstaad?"

"I don't know. But he left in a hurry, so he must have just received information from someone."

"From whom? Not Raoul."

"So Raoul has information."

"No. No. It was just a way of talking."

"You did, didn't you? You did take money."

"Horst. Don't be crazy. Matt doesn't know what he is talking about." Andre's voice did not sound very convincing.

"Tell me straight out that you did not take the funds from your bank."

"Horst. How could you believe that I would do such a thing?"

Andre's lack of direct denial was adequate indictment for Horst. "You fucking bastard. I'm holding more than 150,000 shares of USOCO that will go down the drain because of this."

"Horst. Please. You've nothing to worry about. I have everything under control."

"What do you mean 'control'. Matt is on his way to Garweiler. How do you intend to control that?"

"Listen to me. Matt will not reach Garweiler."

"How precisely do you intend to stop him?"

"Eh, Garweiler is in Gstaad. I will see him first and tell

him the whole story."

"And have Garweiler all over your bank on Monday. Somehow I doubt that you will do that."

"Then let's just say that I will get to Matt first."

"You'd better. Or I'll get to you."

Horst slammed down the phone. He sat in the phone booth a minute and then went out to his guests. They were gathered around a table in preparation for the buffet luncheon. For the most part they were thoroughly enjoying each other's company and entirely oblivious to Horst's absence. Horst approached them holding his right arm with his left hand.

"Horst, we congratulate you on your excellent horsemanship," said one of the bankers who had not even left the bar to watch the events.

"Thank you," said Horst, seemingly having regained his composure. "But as you can see, I have sprained my wrist. They have advised me to go to the hospital to have it X-rayed."

"Ooh," said the group in unison, most of them wondering if that meant they would have to leave as well.

"But you gentlemen are most welcome to stay. Please help yourself to anything you need, and simply charge it to me."

The group around the table raised their glasses of altbier and wished him well. It was evident that before he had even exited the room that they had forgotten about him, nor even noticed that he had already let go of his arm.

Horst then went to the tackhouse. He opened his tackbox and reached for the luger. When he noticed it was not there he turned to Herr Barnum.

"Has anyone been in my box today?"

"Yes, that American you sent to pick up something you forgot. Is there something missing?"

Horst began to curse at the tackmaster, but held back.

"No. No. It is okay. I forgot about that."

Horst picked up the rifle and the shotgun, some rounds of ammunition and put them in his car. He drove home, changed out of his riding clothes and into slacks, a heavy wool pullover, and an Antartex sheepskin jacket. He pulled out a map from the glove compartment and marked out a route leading southward to Switzerland. He estimated that it should take him about eight hours of fast driving to reach his destination.

After hanging up with Horst, Andre dialed Raoul's number in Geneva. Not to Andre's surprise, Raoul was at home, surrounded by numerous bookkeeping and accounting ledgers.

"Raoul," said Andre. "I think we have trouble."

"How so?" asked Raoul. "Aren't the books in balance?"

"It's not the books. I think someone is on to us."

"Christine," responded Raoul, almost automatically.

"No. Why do you say Christine? I am thinking of someone else."

Raoul repeated the details of the incident in the office. Andre was silent for a moment.

"Ah. It is beginning to come together. I think I know how Matt Allyn got on our trail."

"Allyn -- but I don't understand. What could he know?"

"That's what I was wondering. But if what you tell me about Christine is true, she must be the connection."

"Merde." Raoul started to show visible signs of tension. "What should I do?"

"Can you find Christine?"

"I can try calling her at her apartment."

"Good. Call me back as soon as you have found out something."

Raoul hung up the phone and reached for the telephone book. He nervously thumbed through the pages until he reached the Evins listing. He dialled her number. No answer. He wondered if he should go to her apartment to wait. But she could be away for the weekend and he would foolishly be sitting outside for hours waiting her return. He called Andre back.

"There's no answer at her apartment and I don't know where else to look."

"Okay then. Hold tight until you can reach her. Allyn may come here. I'll be watching on this end."

Raoul hung up the phone and poured a cognac to steady his nerves. Oh God, he thought, why couldn't You have just waited until Tuesday.

CHAPTER FORTY TWO

Matt saw Christine slumped over in a chair in the lobby of the hotel when he arrived. She looked the worst he had ever seen her -- her face was pale to the point of ashen, her hair was rumpled and she wore no makeup. Her eyes were half closed. She wore faded jeans and an old cardigan sweater which she had wrapped tightly around her torso. A suede coat lined with sheepskin had been tossed beside her. She had to have been sitting in the lobby chair since they spoke, he thought, for her to seem so lifeless.

He was practically on top of her by the time she realized he had arrived.

"Oh, Matt. I'm so happy to see you. I could not have handled this alone."

"It's all right. We'll work it out together. You wait here while I register."

When Matt finished with the formalities they went upstairs to his room. Partly to save time, partly to insure privacy, Matt declined the bellhop and carried his own bags. Christine was carrying a school bookbag, a leftover from her university days. Other spectators in the lobby watched the pair curiously, as if in agreement that the two made a decidely incongruous couple.

After entering the room Matt threw his luggage to one side and moved towards Christine. As curious as he was about the papers, he was even more interested in her touch. He kissed her softly. She was very responsive, as if she were hungering for a positive feeling after the series of negative emotions she had been suffering. Matt started to caress her body more intensely.

"No, no. Not now. You have to look at these papers first. You have to tell me if I am crazy or not."

Christine disengaged herself from Matt's hold and went over to her bookbag. Out of it she pulled a package of duplicated papers, which she had segregated into different groups with paperclips. She laid them down on the hotel room desk, and beckoned for Matt to have a seat.

"These are the ones that I got from Raoul's office. Each page represents a different customer's account. You see, they are all losing money."

Matt looked at the pages without any comment.

"Now these are copies of computer statements taken from the same customers' file at the bank. You see, on these statements, each customer shows a gain."

"But in different investments."

"Yes, but you see, I don't know which investments are real. And why would Raoul keep records of losing transactions?"

Good question, thought Matt. "Who inputs the data into the computer."

"Mostly by the office clerks. But Raoul designed the

computer, and he has an access terminal in his office."

Matt wondered if it were possible to phony up every customer's account. He remembered the Equity Funding case, in which the 'boys' in the computer room had created a whole series for fraudulent insurance policies for years without being detected.

"How many customers does LeFevre have?" Matt asked.

"About 1,000. But only about 200 of them have substantial portfolios -- some of them in the hundreds of millions. And I found copies of all their files in Raoul's drawers."

"Well, I can't say that it is so damning yet. Maybe he keeps records on trades that he considered doing, but didn't."

"Maybe. But look at this. This is material that I found in one of the drawers in Andre's office. It shows all kinds of losses that the bank took over the last five years. Look, losses in foreign exchange, in gold, in real estate, in the stock market. If the bank took so many losses, why didn't it show up on the customer's account?"

"Maybe they were losses on the bank's own capital."

"But I see the figures before they go to the Directors. We have always reported a gain."

Matt shifted uneasily in his chair. The documents were definitely not comforting. But they provided an explanation as to why Andre was attempting to greenmail USOCO. The money they made on the scam would be adequate to refund the losses they had taken over the years, and to put the bank back on a solvent footing. A desperate move on Andre's part, but the bank appeared to be in a desperate position.

198

"I think you are right. But there is still not enough evidence. What you have is handwritten portfolios and sheets of paper showing losses in trading activity. It suggests a lot of possibilities, but it doesn't prove that Andre or Raoul has been cooking the books."

"Cooking the books?" Christine did not understand Matt's lingo.

"You know, changing the numbers to make a more palatable dish for the Directors."

"Yes, I'm now sure that that's it. Andre LeFevre still lives in the shadow of his father. He doesn't believe he can live up to his father's successes, and is more afraid to admit his failures."

"I think we should go to the banking authorities."

"You mean Hans Garweiler?"

"Yes. But the only problem is that by the time they complete their investigation, it might be too late."

"Too late for what?"

"The payoff. LeFevre is to receive a substantial amount of money on Tuesday in payment for his share holdings. You see, he has greenmailed a company -- threatening to engineer a takeover by an Arab unless the company pays them to call off the transaction. By Tuesday, LeFevre will have won -- they will effectively have stolen money from USOCO."

"If we could prove that LeFevre were stealing money, would they close it down immediately?"

"Yes, but what you have here is pretty suspicious, but it

isn't proof."

"I think I know where Andre keeps the proof."

"Really. Where?"

"In the top drawer of his credenza in his office."

"Can we get it?"

"I don't have the key. We would have to force it open."

Matt thought for a moment. With no proof, there was really no case. He has nothing concrete for the Central Bank. There was not enough reason to bring it to their attention -- and certainly no reason to do anything before Tuesday. Matt sighed. The deal would be saved.

He looked at Christine. "Well, we can't break into his office just to get some papers that may or may not be there -- that would be against the law."

"But isn't what he is doing even worse."

"Why. He stands to make a bundle on the deal -- repay back everything he 'borrowed', and have a pile of money left over. Actually, the whole scheme is brilliant."

"And you make your money too. Right. Would you be so reluctant to pursue this if you had nothing to gain?"

"Christine, you have to understand my position."

"I do," she said softly. "I understand it very well."

Matt sat rigid in his chair, staring ahead. Finally, he turned and looked at her.

"Well, what are we waiting for?" he said.

CHAPTER FORTY THREE

Fifteen minutes later Matt and Christine left the hotel. Christine had spent a few minutes fixing her face and hair -- she wanted to be sure the story they had concocted for the bank guard looked plausible. Matt carried an attache case. He was still dressed in the same outfit he had been in since he left Germany, except that he took the luger out of his luggage and put it in his blazer pocket. He was quite conscious of its weight and the cold hard feeling against his body. It gave him more of a sense of gloom than that of security.

Christine attempted to smooth her wind ruffled hair as they approached the bank's door. She pushed the buzzer next to the heavy door. After several rings, the guard came to the door. It was not Herr Ringgli as she had hoped, but one that Christine had only seen occasionally. Christine searched her memory for his name.

"The bank is closed," he said in a disinterested voice.

"Monsieur Goddot." Christine wondered if she had picked the right name.

"Yes."

"You remember me, Christine Evins, Mr. LeFevre's secretary."

"Yes. And?"

"Well, something important has come up. May we enter?"

The guard allowed them in past the doors, but blocked their passage to the mainlobby. He was under orders not to let anyone enter who had not put his name on a list the night before.

"What is the problem?"

"This gentleman is Mr. Allyn. He is here in Geneva from New York. We, that is, I, was supposed to have sent him a power of attorney to his hotel so he could conclude a deal today in Geneva. But I forgot. So he had to call me at home to remind me. I have the papers upstairs on my desk. He would like to pick it up."

The guard eyed her suspiciously -- Christine suspected that he would not know a power of attorney from a will. Finally, he said, "Okay, you go up. The gentleman can wait here."

"Uh, no. He must come with me," protested Christine, a little too obviously she thought. "There are several papers -- I am not sure which ones are the correct ones, and besides, he must sign the receipts. It would be much easier if he just came along."

"How long will you be?"

"Oh, just a few minutes, I am sure."

"Okay. Go ahead."

The guard watched the two of them go into the elevator, and after the doors shut, he picked up the phone.

"Mr. Hengler? This is M. Goddot, the guard on duty at the bank today. I am calling you because I do not think it's important enough to call M. LeFevre in Gstaad. I just wanted to tell you that Christine Evins has come to the bank with another man. One of the customers. His name? Allain, I think. Is it all right? You will be right over. Very well, I will detain them until you arrive."

Matt and Christine entered Andre's office cautiously, as if somemone were waiting behind the door. As he walked across the threshold, Matt was conscious of his heartbeat quickening -- he looked at Christine -- she too seemed to be breathing more noticeably. He wondered if he had allowed himself to get into something foolish -- would he have thoroughly rejected the notion of embezzlement had it been Whitey showing him the books and not Christine. He thought for a second of just closing the door and walking out -- but Christine's anxious look made him realize that he had to go through with what they started. Hopefully the guard would not become suspicious and start to check them out.

"That's the credenza where I found the loose sheets that showed the losses. I think that all the other books are in the top drawer." said Christine.

As an automatic reaction, Matt pulled at the handle even though Christine had assured him it was locked. There was no give at all. Matt inspected the lock --it was a full tumbler Yale type lock, not the simple ones that are usually on a desk. He pulled out the bottom draw, still stuffed with the records that Christine had duplicated. Carefully he sifted

203

through those. Nothing except the loose sheets that he had already seen. Nothing specifically damning. Matt removed the drawer entirely. He looked up through the open space it left to see if the lock could be manipulated from inside. Clearly not -- each drawer had a separate locking system. Andre must have been careless in not locking the bottom drawer.

"I don't see any way to open this," he said.

"Maybe we can pry it open," answered Christine. She began looking around the room for something to use as leverage.

Christine brought over a letter opener that had been on Andre's desk. Its silver inlaid irovy handle placed it in the eighteenth century.

"It looks a little frail, but we'll give it a try."

Matt made a few cursory pickings at the lock, which proved futile, and then attempted to slide it between the drawer and the credenzas casing. He managed to get the tip in, but when he appliead some leverage pressure the blade snapped. Matt was beginning to feel silly.

"You don't suppose there is a keypick around here?"

"A what?" Christine's English did not include a summary of useful burglar's tools.

Matt just shook his head. "Any other tools around?"

The two looked around the room at the other paraphenalia that lay on the desk and in the large bookcase on the right wall. Matt became conscious of the clutter of antiques that filled Andre's office. On close inspection everything struck Matt to be absolutely useless -- lamps that would never provide lighting, inkwells and antique pens, even the vases would be too fragile to be used for flowers -- as if the owner were deliberately emphasizing the aura of luxury. Certainly nothing that even vaguely resembled a crowbar was to be found.

Christine looked at Matt and shrugeed her shoulders. Matt was equally at a loss. Christine could probably run to a hardware store to get some tools, but how would she get them past the guard, wondered Matt. Then suddenly he turned to Christine.

"I've got an idea. First let's get some cushions from the chairs. Quick," he said.

"Cushions?"

"Yes. Here, help me carry these." Matt was pulling off the cushions from the seats of the two fauteilles. He handed one to Christine and carried one himself over to the credenza. "Hope these aren't antiques."

Matt arranged the two on the top front edge of the credenza in the front. He carefully marked where he thought the locking device on the piece of furniture would be located under pillows. He then drew out the luger, and aiming very slowly, slot through the cushions at the lock. As Matt had expected, the sound of the shot was muffled, but the sound of the bullet hitting the metal lock was very loud, with a shrill repeat when the bullet ricocheted. Both Matt and Christine jumped back out of automatic reflex. Matt wondered if the noise could be heard three floors below at the guard desk.

They pulled away the cushions and surveyed the shattered lock. Matt pulled at the drawer, which resisted opening because part of the splintered lock had imbedded in the credenza's top. Matt decided to give the lock one more round from the gun. He set the pillows up again as quickly as he could and pulled the trigger, this time more braced for the noise. Nothing happened. Matt squeezed again again only a click. Matt pulled the gun away and opened the magazine. Empty. No clip at all inside. The first shot must have been whatever had been automatically loaded into the chamber from the previous clip. What an idiot, he hought to himself -- you stole a gun but no bullets. He threw the pistol on top of Andre's desk, gouging the veneer.

Matt attempted again to pull open the drawer but with no success. To get more leverage, Matt braced himself in a stoop position on the floor and gave the drawer several particularly hard jerks. It suddenly flew opened and fell to the floor, causing Matt to fall back against Andre's desk. Christine rushed to Matt's side.

"I'm all right. I'm all right. Let's look at this stuff already." Given all the damage he was creating, Matt hoped to God that the papers would be duly incriminating.

Inside the drawer were several large ledger books, each dated a different year. Matt opened the most recent years. Inside were page after page containing two sets of accounts, with the same headings but different amounts, mostly negative on the left side and mostly positive numbers on the right side. Matt put that book down and picked up the one for the previous year. The same thing was evident. Matt riffled through several other books and then looked up at Christine.

"Christine, my love, I will never doubt your genius again. You are absolutely right. Andre is committing a fraud of the first order."

Christine sighed. "I don't mind your calling me a genius, but I wish it weren't for this reason. I wish you had found old chocolate wrappers in there." She stiffled a sob. One part of her world was slowly unraveling.

"Let's get out of here. I don't want your guard friend to start to get suspicious."

"Where should we go?"

"Where does Hans Garweiler live?"

"Garweiler. I know him. I met him at one of the bank's functions."

"Can you get his address?"

'Yes, it must be in the rolodex file." Christine started to flip through the cards in her desk. She pulled out a card and returned to Andre's office. Matt was still behind the desk.

"Yes I have his address and telephone number here -- he lives in Berne. But I also have a Gstaad address for the weekends, but no telephone number. Oh!"

"What. What's wrong."

"That's where Andre is this weekend."

"So what. That doesn't mean anything. Everybody goes to Gstaad in the winter. Everyone that can afford it, that is."

"I'll check to make sure he's there." Christine dialed the Berne number. The housekeeper answered and confirmed that he was away for the weekend.

"May I have his telephone number there."

"No, Madame, I am specifically forbidden to give out that number. Mr. Garweiler wants his privacy during the weekend."

"But this is very important."

"Yes. They all say that. But I am terribly sorry."

Christine hung up. She looked at Matt.

"It doesn't matter. We would have to show him the books anyway. He wouldn't just believe two idiots like us ranting on the telephone."

"Yes. You're right. Let me write down Garweiler's address in Gstaad." Christine started to reach into Andre's top drawer for a pen and a piece of paper.

"That won't be necessary," said a voice from the doorway to Andre's office.

Christine gasped. "Mr. Hengler." Hengler was standing in the door pointing a revolver at the them.

"I thought something strange was going on with you, Miss Evins. You seemed to be doing a lot of poking around for a little secretary."

Christine didn't reply. Matt responded for her, trying not to sound melodramatic. "You're the one doing all the strange stuff. You and Andre have been juggling the books."

"Never mind what we did. We only need you to arrange the delivery of the stock on Tuesday, and everything will be cleared up."

"There won't be any stock transaction on Tuesday." Matt voice was beginning to have a slight quaver. He hadn't seen a gun pointed at him since Vietnam.

"And why not? There is nothing you can do to stop it."

Raoul's voice had begun to pitch upwards -- Matt suspected that Raoul was as nervous as he.

"Yes. First, we are bringing these books to Garweiler. After that we are calling Kramer at USOCO to tell him that there is no Arab connection. Do you think that you will see moncy after that?"

"Your words sound very good, but how will you turn them into action. You see, I intend to turn you over to the police for burgularizing this office."

"But I will tell them everything." Raoul was quiet for a second. Matt got the impressions that Raoul was playing this whole thing by ear.

"You mean," Raoul finally said, "if you are still alive. I'll tell them I caught you in the act, and had to defend myself. Unfortunate incident."

Christine let out a shrill little sound and then started to squelch it. As Raoul turned his eyes towards her, Matt looked at the empty luger sitting on the desk -- Raoul had apparently not seen it yet. Should he attempt to grab it, he wondered. He even wondered if Raoul's gun were loaded -- the whole bit about defending himself seemed like a bluff. Raoul simply did not have the nerves of a cold blooded killer. Suddenly, Christine started to sway. The lack of sleep, lack of food, and Raoul's scare was getting to her -- she was starting to collapse.

As Raoul instinctively moved towards Christine, Matt grabbed the pistol on the desk and threw it at Hengler. As a reflex, Raoul pulled the trigger on his revover, proving that was indeed loaded. The wild shot missed both Matt and Christine, but the flying gun caught Raoul on the left temple, cracking the glasses as well. The stun knocked him to the floor and the gash started to bleed. He lay there, seemingly unconscious.

Matt looked at Christine. The sound of the revolver had shocked her, and she was now alert. "Oh my God. Matt. What should we do? Should we call the police?"

"No. That will only delay us more. They'd never believe our story anyway. We have to get to Garweiler. Let's just get out of here."

"But what about Raoul."

"I think he is just unconscious. He'll proabably be out for an hour or so."

Matt threw the incriminating books in the attache case while Christine grabbed the overcoats and the rolodex card with Garweiler's address. They ran towards the hall.

"This way," said Christine, "towards the fire stairs. The guard may be coming up the elevator if he heard the shot."

Matt had increasing admiration for Christine's intelligence. When they went down to the lobby, the guard had indeed left his post, but when they reached the front door, it was locked. Matt realized they would be trapped in the building.

"I think I have the key to the front door. It was probably one of the ones that was on Herr Ringgli's key chain."

Christine pulled out several keys on a wire holder, and started trying each one. As Christine expected, one of them worked. They then locked it from the outside, and started to walk away hurriedly, trying not to attract any attention.

Raoul had been stunned by the impact of the gun against his glasses, but he came to much quicker than Matt had expected. Raoul directed the guard to call the police immediately. He would turn the tables and build a criminal case built against the two interlopers, he decided. That would certainly make it easier for Andre to deal with them, with full justification and reason. Common burglars looting valuable antiques from the bank director's private office.

The police, with typical Swiss efficiency arrived quickly, their cars swerving,but completely under control on the now slippery Geneva streets. After the search was completed, Raoul called Andre, and described the situation. "I almost caught them here, but they got away. They have the books and they are going to Garweiler's place."

"Which one?"

"In Gstaad."

"Good".

"Then they will be in my territory. Don't worry. They will never reach Garweiler."

CHAPTER FORTY FOUR

At the corner, Matt and Christine paused for a moment to catch their breath. The cold air felt raw and numbing. Matt looked at Christine -- she looked more fatigued than ever. He knew that she had hardly eaten or slept in the last twenty-four hours.

"Listen." said Matt. "Why don't you go home. It's probably better to call the police anyway. Then we'll straighten this out without a cops and robbers escapade.

Christine was exhausted, but she knew that had to get through to Matt that this was not New York and that his civil rights were not going to be treated in the same manner by the Swiss -- who viewed every foreigner with grave suspicion, including the Pope.

"Matt, you're very naive. Do you really think that once the police are informed by Andre LeFevre, one of the most prominent citizens of Geneva, that an American stocckbroker has illegally entered his bank, burglarized his office, shot a hole in his private safe, stole papers and assaulted his trusted assistant -- do you really think that the police are going to listen to your crazy story?

"We have no choice. We have got to get a car and drive straight to Herr Garweiler's weekend chalet in Gstaad. He is one of the most honorable men in Switzerland. You might say he is a Swiss Paul Volcker -- just as incorruptable -- I'm sure he'll listen to us. He'll know me because I met him at the bank. If we can only get to him our problems will be over."

Matt sighed. "I hope you're right, Christine. But there is a lot of money involved here -- and a lot of greed."

Matt gathered up his energy. "All right. But we better get some wheels. How about a Hertz Rent a Car? I'm sure they'll put me in the driver's seat."

Christine thought for a moment, and then shook her head. "I can't think right now. I don't know where one is -- I don't rent cars, I always take the train."

"Well, I'm sure there's one at the airport. Let's get a cab here before people start to notice us."

At the airport, Matt arranged for the car while Christine waited in a nearby chair, her eyes half closed. After finishing with the rental agency, he left her there while he went to a nearby food concession. While the Swiss do not have fast food take out, he was able to manage to get the concession lady to put the saucisson on some bread and to wrap it with paper. He also picked out some apples, a juice drink for Christine and coffee for himself. He carried them over to Christine, and then went in search of a telephone.

He direct dialled a long number in New York.

"Whitey. I'm calling from Geneva. There's something going on here."

"Something to do with USOCO, I'll bet."

"Why do you say that?"

"Because there's a big article in the Times about the

Arabs tendering for USOCO at $75 a share. I thought LeFevre was selling out."

"He is. That article is all just part of the scam."

"What do you mean, 'scam'?"

"Hold on to your cock. Just like we thought, there is no big Arab buyer. But how did our friend get the money? It turns out that LeFevre has been embezzling his bank's own customer funds to buy the stock."

"Are you positive?"

"Yes. I have all the papers to prove it." Matt outlined the day's events.

"Un-fucking-believable."

"Isn't it. I've been a real idiot in this. I should have figured it out a long time ago."

"But we didn't do anything wrong."

"I agree. But we can't let that stock be delivered to USOCO on Tuesday. The whole thing's a fraud."

"Have you spoken to Kramer?"

"No. I don't have his number. Maybe you can try to reach him. We have the company's number at the office."

"I'll do my best." Whitey sounded despondent. "Why does our best customer have to turn out to be a shithead."

"Yeah. Better smart than lucky next time."

Matt went back to Christine. She had finished her food and was gathering up the baggage. They went to the allotted car and got in. He ate while Christine doubled checked the route to Gstaad. Connversation had dribbled down to just a few mandatory words. By the time Matt pulled out on the highway leading towards Lausanne, Christine was asleep.

At the same time, Andre LeFevre sat quietly in the living room of his chalet drinking scotch. In the fireplace, additional logs had been thrown on the burning cinders, giving off an unusual heat. Andre's face had become flushed. Despite his active mental state, he was outwardly calm and his movements slow and deliberate. His wife entered the room.

"Andre," she said, "it's time to get ready to go to the Schneider's."

Andre turned towards her. "I'm not going. You should go alone."

"What. Why aren't you coming?"

"Because I don't want to." He looked at her without the slightest trace of expression in his face. "But I want you to go. And take the white Mercedes."

"Are you all right?"

"Yes. Just tired. Now go!" The last part was said with such vigor that his wife virtually fled the room. Andre remained in the room. After a period of time he got up, walked to a closet in the hall, pulled out a small wooden box, and removed a mauser pistol. He opened the magazine and put in a new clip. He lookd at the clock. It was 9:00 PM. If Matt and Christine left Geneva when Raoul called, they should be in Gstaad between 10 and 11 PM. He would start his vigil before ten o'clock, just in case.

One hour later, Andre pulled the black Peugeot 504 that his wife normally uses and drove to the road that leads to the

Garweiler chalet. He knew that the white car would have stood out among the dark trees that lined the road, but a black car would be camoflaged very well. A few chalets clustered at the point wherethe road met with the main town street, but higher up, where Garweiler's chalet was, the road was virtually deserted. Only one driveway, Garweiler's, intersected with the road, but the chalet that it led to 500 yards further lay out of sight. A small marker, with the letters HG, stuck in the road's shoulder immediately before the driveway was the only indication of chalet's owner.

Andre parked his car on the far side of a large fir that grew just past the entry to the Garweiler driveway. He shut the engine, turned off his lights, got out and walked up the driveway. About 100 yards from the house he stopped. He could see one car parked in the drive, which he recognized to be Garweiler's. Beyond he could see the chalet with several lights burning. He had hoped that Garweiler would not be there, but was pleased that Matt and Christine had apparently not yet arrived. He returned to his own car and began his wait, turning on the engine occasionally to provide some warmth.

Christine began to wake about two hours later, as Matt was starting up the mountain roads. It was very dark with intermittent snow. Christine was wearing boots, but Matt still had on the outfit that he had put on that morning for Horst's affair, gray slacks, a blue blazer and his Ferragamo slip-ons. He hoped for the sake of both his feet and his shoes that he would not have to tromp around in much snow.

The driving was becoming difficult. Matt was beginning to feel his own limited sleep -- his eyes always tired first, and the glare caused by the snow and the oncoming traffic was beginning to really bother him. He would have liked to stop and spend the night at any of the inns they passed on the highway, and find Garweiler in the morning. But he realized that the police would probably be on his tail by now.

Hengler might have told them that they were off to Gstaad --
it would be easy to track them down at any hotel since he
would have to show his passport to register. Pushing on
was the only option.

As Christine stirred Matt reached out and squeezed her
hand. Suddenly the car started a skid as he rounded a curve.
He quickly pulled his hand back and steered out of the skid.
The car righted itself, but the action shook Matt. He turned
off the road on to the next quiet drive and stopped the car.
The two sat still for a minute. Matt reached over to Christine
and kissed her.

"I must look like a wreck," she said.

"You look just fine to me," replied Matt, sliding down in
her arms. "Outside of a good meal and a soft bed, you are all
I want right now."

"Oh, Matt. I wish we didn't have to do this."

"You wish. Matthew Allyn, combat broker, that's me.
Yesterday I was sitting in New York, writing orders for
stocks and bonds. Today I'm on the trail of an international
financial thief. Christine, you've shown me a lifestyle I
never expected to see."

Christine laughed. Matt was pleased to hear it -- he was
especially fond of her when she laughed. He sunk down
further in her arms, almost in her lap. he was about to
embrace her once more for a kiss, when he heard a loud
siren. A police car passed within seconds on the main road.

"Do you think they are after us," Christine asked.

"I have no idea," Matt answered. "But let's not wait
around to find out. They are ahead of us now, so we should
be safe for a while."

Matt started up the engine again and went back to the

main road. The climbs became steeper and the road more winding. Occasionally Matt cracked the window to get a blast of the cold air. The signs pointing to Gstaad became more frequent, and just as Matt felt that he couldn't have gone much further, they entered the town limits.

They stopped at one of the hotels and asked for directions to the road that led to the Garweiler chalet. The two used the hotel facilities to freshen up, returned to the car and started their drive.

"It's now 10:45. So we should be there in fifteen minutes," said Christine.

"If we don't get lost. I can barely see the entrances to the side roads."

"I'm not worried about that. I'm more worried that he won't be there. Or that he will be asleep, or that he won't believe us."

"Oh, he'll believe us after what we have to show him." Matt was bginning to feel a little more revived. "I think our worries will be soon over."

CHAPTER FORTY FIVE

That Saturday morning, Jack McGrory woke later than usual. The winter sun had not yet be able to penetrate the strong cloud cover. Even though it was 9:00 AM, it still felt like nighttime. Jack was bleary eyed and had a pounding headache. The previous night he had had more than his usual quota of Chivas. The last few weeks had been very trying for Jack -- his losses had reached $18 million -- another $2 million down would force him to seek a merger partner with a stronger specialist firm. The Stock Exchange had put his firm on their watch list -- the first time he had ever come close to being in technical violation of the capital requirements.

His current position was short two million shares. That meant that if the stock rose one more point on Tuesday, from the current level of $56, he would be in very deep trouble. Slipping on a bright red silk robe, which made his eyes squint, Jack went to the kitchen, poured a cup of coffee that his wife had left in the automatic brewer, opened the service door in his apartment and picked up the morning copy of the New York Times. As he looked at the front page, the coffee cup slippped out of his hand and crashed to the floor. The worst case scenario was laid out before him in 24 point type.

The lower right hand column had a special lead picked up from the London Economic Times.

"Arab Swiss Consortium to Begin Tender Offer for 100% of USOCO Shares. Price of $75 per Share Indicated." The story went on to say that a group of wealthy sheiks from Dubai, a Gulf Coast Emirate, had already accumulated over the past six months a significant position in the stock, through Andre LeFevre & Co., a prominent private Swiss bank. The story further said that the USOCO management has yet to comment on the proposed tender offer, and that attempts to contact the CEO Herbert Kramer had been unsuccessful.

Jack's stomach started churning. This was the end of the world as far as he was concerned. In thirty years on the floor, he had seen the coming of the end of the world seventeen times, but this time it would really happen. There was no escape. He ran to the bathroom, and put his head into the toilet. He wretched violently, his empty stomach producing little more than dry heaves.

Igor, Max Adler's tiger striped cat, jumped up on Max's bed to wake him. Max stroked the top of his cat's head and rubbed behind its ears as he eagerly purred. Looking out of his bedroom window, Max could see the Long Island Sound stretched out before him. Max's house was suited to a wealthy Wall Streeter, a large tudor sytle affair hidden behind high walls on Beech Avenue in Westport, Connecticut.

Outside his bedroom on a tray lay the morning newspapers, and a glass of freshly squeezed orange juice, laid there eariler that morning by his chauffer/handyman. Max got up, washed his face, picked up the tray and returned to his room. The rest of the morning would be devoted to reading the news and to his cat.

After returning to bed, Max opened the Times first. He skimmed the top half and flipped to the lower section. The USOCO article stared him in the face. Max was not given to displays of emotion, except when a big hit in the market was scored. He let out a whoop -- he had struck gold again. Mentally he ran down the total holdings accumulated by him and his partners. They owned 3.5 million shares at an average cost of $42 a share. That means that every share would earn $20. Multiplied by 3.5 million, the syndicate would gross $70 million dollars.

The phone rang. It was Marty Fishbein, the one who had begged Max to sell him out early. Marty had akso read the article.

"Max. Max." whined Marty. "Okay, you were right as always. Next time I'll listen."

"Marty, you're a great guy. But my investors have the courage of my convictions. Sorry, Marty, there won't be a next time. You've been struck off the list."

It was a crowded holiday weekend in Manchester, Vermont, where Jon Smathers and Betsy were taking a three day ski vacation. It had been snowing heavily all morning, and the visibility on the slopes was close to zero. It was expected to clear for the afternoon, so most skiers were in the base lodge at Bromley waiting for the snow to stop. Jon and Betsy were sitting at one of the long wooden tables near the window drinking hot chocolate. It was a typcial base lodge -- filled with the noise of clomping ski boots and screaming kids, and humid enough to steam the lens of eye glasses. Smathers and Betsy had run out of conversation but reading in that atmosphere was impossible. So the two sat silently watching the passing parade.

Bored, Smathers got up and went to the main level to see if the newspaper vending machines had received any of the big city editions. The New York Times was just being loaded in. Smathers picked up a copy, folded it under his arm and went to rejoin Betsy. He started to open it to read, but Betsy stopped him.

"You can't read in here -- besides, I'm really getting bored. The snow is slowing down. Why don't we go for a few runs."

Smathers refolded the paper and put it in his rucksack. The two left the lodge and went towards the lift leading to the Lord's Prayer slope, one of Bromley's more difficult runs.

Smathers didn't open the paper until they reached their motel room. Betsy had gone in to take her shower -- Smathers decided to skim it while waiting. Out of habit, he turned to the business section first, which had no articles of particular interest. Then he turned back to look at the front page headlines. There he saw the USOCO story -- he knew the implications immediately. His total $50,000 option speculation would turn into a cool $400,000 profit come the opening of trading Tuesday morning. He jumped up and ran into the bathroom.

"Bets," he shouted over the streaming water. He started to take off his clothes.

"What? What's wrong?" Betsy hadn't ever seen Smathers so excited.

Smathers opened the sliding glass doors and pushed his way into the shower.

"I did it, Bets. I won with the USOCO options. I told you I would be right and I was." Smathers turned his face towards the shower head, letting the water rush over his head. Then he turned to Bets, put one arm around her waist and the other between her legs.

"Does this mean we'll be getting married soon?"

"Yeah, Bets, soon," he said, as his fingers groped deeper.

Nick Bianco was sitting in his den in his home in Essex Fells, New Jersey, a suburban community they moved to after his income was big enough to get him out of Brooklyn. He was half watching a cable rebroadcast of the Knicks game, half reading Barrons, the weekly financial newspaper which comes out on Saturday. Both together were not adequate to keep his mind filled. For all the comforts of home, he would rather be in the small apartment on the West Side with Carol. He hadn't read the Times yet -- the Saturday edition isn't delivered to his home, and it was snowing too hard to bother to drive to pick it up.

The phone rang. His wife answered it and called to him to pick up. It was Jimbo.

"Nick -- did you see the Times this morning?"

"No," responded Nick, rather dully. "I haven't been out. Why? Anything in it?"

"You kidding me. How about $75 a share for USOCO from the Arabs in a takeover bid."

"No shit! Bingo! Shit, I knew I was right. Thanks for telling me. I've got to go get the paper."

Nick hung up the phone and started to swing his arms around like a wild boxer. His energy level was soaring. He held his arms over his head like Rocky after winning a match. His wife came into the room.

"What's up?"

"Big win in the market. We did it. Holy shit." He grabbed her around the waist and started to swing her around.

"Nick, don't do that. I've got cooking on the stove."

"Yeah. Okay." Nick slowed down. "Look, I've got to go to New York for a while"

"Now? Why?"

"Eh, to meet with Jimbo and some other guys about our strategy on the stock. Big movement coming up in the price"

His wife had next to no idea about the stock market, which he relied on whenever he needed an excuse.

"When will you be back? I'm making a big dinner for tonight."

"Don't worry. I'll be back for dinner." Nick put on his overcoat and headed for the door.

Nick drove to the local grocery store, picked up a Times, paid the shopkeeper, and read the article while still in the store. He then went to the phone booth in the back and dialled a New York number.

"Carol. Get your ass in gear, Baby, cause I'm going to be there in thirty minutes and I'm going to ball you like you've never been balled before."

Herb Kramer had just put down the phone. Being in Texas he normally didn't get the New York Times, which had to be ordered specially to reach his home in Houston. But Owen Perry had heard from a friend in New York that there was a big article, so he picked it up and called Kramer as soon as he read it. Kramer did not take the news very well.

"Goddam bastards. What kind of a fucking game are they playing? They'll get their lousy $65 a share. Mother fucking shit kickers," he said out loud. His heart was beginning to pump. He was glad that his wife was not in the room -- she would be clucking all around him.

He debated whether to call LeFevre directly to pass along his opinion of LeFevre tactics. He picked up the phone and laid it down. What was the point? LeFevre would be out of his hair by Tuesday, and this article only supported his claim to the Board that these poeple were undesirable. He started to calm down. The phone rang again.

"Yeah," said Kramer, expecting that it was Owen Perry again.

'Hello, Mr. Kramer."

"Yes. Who is this?" Kramer did not like to hear unfamiliar vices over the phone.

"This is Ted Whitehill. I'm with Matthew Allyn and Co. I have some news regarding LeFevre & Cie."

Damn, thought Kramer, these guys don't stop. "What do you want?"

"My partner, Matthew Allyn, just called from Geneva. It seems there may be some trouble with their stock tender."

"Trouble?" More greenmail, thought Kramer. He was starting to sweat. "What kind of trouble?"

"Well, my partner was not very specific, but he feels there may be some irregularities in the way the accumulation was handled. He is bringing the matter to the attention of the Swiss authorities."

Kramer was speechless. "Are you telling me that this is a fraud."

"Quite possibly. In any case, we suggest that you don't take any action on the buyout until you have heard further from us."

"When will we hear?"

"Hopefully Monday by the latest. Monday's not a holiday in Switzerland and we should have some official word by then."

"We'll be waiting. Call me here anytime, day or night."

Kramer hung up the phone and called Owen Perry.

"Owen, I just heard some more news from LeFevre's New York brokerage firm." Kramer outlined the conversation. "Here's what I want you to do. First, get the Board together for a meeting on Monday at my house. Second, start drafting up a press release denying the takeover stories. And third, get a hold of the New York Stock Exchange. We're going to request a stop trading order as of Tuesday morning."

CHAPTER FORTY SIX

Matt and Christine reached the entry to the road leading to Garweiler's drive.

"This is it," said Christine. "It's just about a mile up this road."

"You know, Matt" she said, as Matt swung the curve. "We haven't thought about Andre."

"What about Andre?"

"What's to prevent him from saying that these documents are nonsense."

"Well, Garweiler should be able to see through that. Andre's not that charming."

"Maybe he's already gotten to Garweiler," she responded. "Raoul might have called him."

"I don't think so. He would be taking a big chance to even raise the subject. What if we weren't really on our way to see him. Garweiler would become very suspicious."

"I guess you're right. We shouldn't be worrying about Andre. He can't do us any harm now."

Christine started watching for driveway entrances. The snow on the road had crusted over, making driving up the steep hill even more treacherous. After several false turns, she saw a drive with a little sticker with the letters HG on it. "This must be it," she said. "Turn here."

LeFevre had been waiting for more than two hours. The cold and the sitting had begun to numb him. He wished that he had brought a flask with cognac. Suddenly he saw lights from the lower part of the road which appeared to be coming from a car. Better be them, he thought. His muscles tightened and his breathing became quicker. He picked up the Mauser, double checked the clip, and put it in his pocket.

The on coming car began to slow as it neared Garweiler's driveway. He could see Christine peering out the window. The car had slowly begun to turn into the drive when Andre jumped out of the Peugeot and ran in front of Matt's car.

"Matt," cried Christine. "It's Andre LeFevre." Matt was too surprised to respond.

"Stop!" shouted Andre. Matt stopped the car and rolled down the window.

"Get out of the way, Andre, we're going to see Garweiler."

"I don't think that's a good idea. What's going on in my bank is none of your concern." replied Andre.

Matt gunned the accelerator, hoping that Andre would be smart enough to get out of the way. But instead the car stood still as the wheels spun in the snow. Andre moved down to Christine's door.

"Lock your door, Christine," shouted Matt, but it was too late. Andre had already pulled the door open. He placed the Mauser next to Christine's head and yanked her out of the car.

"Now I think you better listen to me. I want the books you stole from my office and I intend to get them." Andre's suave demeanor had disappeared, replaced by strident anger.

Matt jumped out of the car. "I don't think that's possible. You'd be a fool to make matters worse. Let Christine go."

"I'll let her go when you give me the books."

"I intend to bring them to Garweiler."

"Okay, Matt. I'll make a deal with you. You give me the books, I'll let Christine go now. And to make sure that you don't turn back, after the sale of the USOCO stock, we'll not only give you the regular $1 million in commissions, but I'll also give you another $1 million on top of that."

Matt looked at Christine -- her eyes revealed fear, but nothing else. She had spent weeks uncovering this fraud -- should he accept being bought off, he wondered. What would she think of him. Christine returned his look, then slowly began to shake her head.

Matt was torn. What would he tell Whitey. Sorry Whitey, we could have made $2 million all together, but Christine didn't think it was right.

LeFevre could see Matt's indecision. "I'll even make it

$2 million on top -- that'll be $3 million in total."

Oh, God, thought Matt. Why can't life be simple.

"Look," said Andre. "I'm not stealing from anyone. Everyone is going to get rich -- I'm not taking anything from my clients. Why must you ruin it just when everything was going so well? If you give me the books, no one, I mean no one, will be hurt. If you don't, every one loses."

Andre was right, thought Matt. No one, least of all Andre's clients, would win by his turning over the books to Garweiler. But it wasn't right. Andre was emblezzling from his own bank. How much stood to go into his own pocket, Matt wondered. Besides, what about USOCO -- they certainly stood to lose -- and to lose big. And what about the innocent shareholders -- don't they count at all?.

"I'm sorry, Andre," said Matt softly. "That's not my way of doing business. It's wrong and you know it."

"I'm sorry for you. I'm going to have to change your plans. I'm going to take you back to my chalet, and tell the police I caught you burglarizing my home. That and your stupid caper at the bank should be adequate to keep you on ice for a while."

"But we'll tell them about the embezzlement," said Christine.

"With what evidence? All our books are in order. Raoul has seen to that. You see this whole exercise was a waste of time. I was willing to give you two million. Now you still can't accomplish your mission, and you get nothing besides. Too bad."

Matt realized he was powerless. The car separated him from Andre and Christine, meaning that he could not even attempt to rush him. Maybe another opportunity would appear to him.

"How do you plan to get us back to your chalet," asked Matt. "We're not just going to get in the back of your car and go for a ride."

"Simple." He yanked Christine by the arm and brought her around to Matt's side of the car, still holding the gun to her head. When he was in arm's reach distance of Matt, he stopped.

"Turn around," he snapped. Matt didn't move. He wanted to see if Andre was really the heavy he pretended to be.

"I said, turn around." Andre turned the aim of the Mauser towards Matt's chest. Matt could see the veins in Andre's forehead, stressed with tension. He realized that Andre was crazed enough to carry through his threat. Christine squealed. Andre's grip on Christine was clearly hurting her.

Matt slowly turned. Was Andre planning to shoot him in the back, he wondered. He felt a sharp pain in his gut, followed by a rush of blood. He was beginning to sweat despite the cold. Matt recognized the sensation from his experiences in Vietnam -- it was that of sheer terror.

CHAPTER FORTY SEVEN

When Matt had fully turned around, Andre raised his gun to land a blow on Matt's head. He would have delivered it had not car lights down the road become visible. Garweiler, thought Andre. So he wasn't at home after all. Andre pulled back the gun, and placed it in Christine ribs.

"Turn around and stand in front of me. Act natural or dear Christine is dead." Matt turned and took the position, hiding Andre's gun from view. The car came up the hill, but the headlight's were too bright for any of the three to see inside. Andre began plotting his excuses.

The car stopped and the driver emerged. It took a while for the three of them to realize that it was not Garweiler.

"Horst," said Matt and LeFevre, almost in unison.

Horst's face was drawn and pale as if he were suffering from a long illness. Matt could not believe that this was the robust looking person he had seen eariler that day. His eyes were staring intently on them. Cradled in his right arm was the shotgun. Matt realized that the way the three were grouped, one shot would hit them all.

"I was hoping to find you." Matt couldn't determine if the comment was directed at him or LeFevre.

"How did you know where to come," asked LeFevre.

"I met Garweiler at your party, remember. He told me where he lived. I take it you haven't had an opportunity to visit with him yet."

"No," said Andre, "and if you hadn't shown up just now, everything would have been taken care of."

"I had to make sure you wouldn't bungle this, Andre." Matt could hear the tension in Horst's voice. "You don't seem to have done a good job with your own bank."

"My bank is my affair."

"It's my affair if that stock price falls."

"It won't. Our friends will be out of sight until after the payoff."

Matt decided to interject. "There won't be any payoff. I've already alerted Kramer at USOCO. He knows the whole story. He's retracting his bid. The takeover frenzy will be over."

Andre and Horst stared at Matt.

"You're bluffing for time," Andre finally said.

"No, I called him from the airport in Geneva. He's going to stop trading on the Exchange Tuesday morning."

"Tuesday," said Horst. "Then I'll sell all my shares on Monday."

"The market isn't open on Monday. It's a national holiday."

Horst stood stock still, his eyes frozen on Andre. "You got me to buy that stock. You told me that nothing could go wrong."

LeFevre didn't answer. Horst's anger was beginning to frighten him.

"I took money from the bank's account because of you. If he finds out, he'll kill me." Horst's voice had raised a full tone, to the point of shrill.

Matt was beginning to understand Horst's fear. He too had embezzled funds to play USOCO. The last 100,000 shares he bought at $ 51 must have been done without his father's blessing. That must be the "he" that Horst was referring to. Matt quickly estimated that Horst stood to lose $2 million dollars if the stock dropped back to $30.

"Horst," said Matt. "Be reasonable. Your father won't hurt you."

Matt had said the wrong thing -- the word 'father' was apparently an anethema to Horst. He began to mumble the same phrase over and over. "He'll kill me. He'll kill me."

"Horst. Please. Stop. It's not that bad." Instinctively, forgetting about Andre's gun, he moved towards Horst.

"Get back," shouted Horst at Matt. "You're just as bad as he is. All you care about is your fucking commissions. You don't care what happens to your customers. You don't give a shit if we all are ruined by your goddam stock market. You're all a bunch of fucking bastards."

Horst's eyes were beginning to widen, and Matt could

234

see Horst bringing the gun up to aim. Matt grabbed Christine's arm and wrenched her down on the ground, Matt falling on top of her for protection. Horst pulled the trigger -- shot sprayed out of the gun. Another shot rang out immediately afterwards.

LeFevre fell backwards on to the snow, his chest riddled with tiny holes. As he fell, he must have pulled the trigger on the Mauser, firing a wild shot. Horst was apparently not hit. He moved towards the three laying on the ground and bent over Andre. Matt started to rise from his position. He couldn't tell if Andre were dead. Horst began to whimper.

Horst grabbed the Mauser from Lefevre's hand and turned towards Matt. Christine was still lying on the ground. Matt realized that the two of them were next in line.

"Horst," cried Matt. "Don't make it any worse for you. At least you can say you killed Andre in self defense -- but don't kill us in cold blood."

Horst was still whimpering -- his nerves were evidently gone. He looked at both of them, and at Andre's body and started to back away in the direction of his car, keeping the gun pointed at Matt. Matt's words had evidently made sense to him, which only added to his confusion. He pulled open the door to his car and, sat inside, with one leg still outside the door.

Matt realized that he and Christine were out of danger, but wondered what Horst thought his next move would be. Was he simply going to drive away, back to Dusseldorf? Matt approached the car. As he did, he could see Horst raising the pistol -- not at Matt, but at his own head.

Matt rushed towards the car and pushed against the door. The pressure of the closing door on Horst's leg caused Horst to scream with pain. Matt reached inside to grab the gun.

235

Horst shoved out of the car, gun still in his right hand, and pushed his left hand into Matt's face. Matt was pushed backwards, but did not fall down. Horst moved away fom the car door and raised the gun again -- this time at Matt.

"Goddammit, Horst. What the hell are you trying to prove? Killing won't make anything else better."

Horst started to lower the gun -- Matt took the cue and threw his body against Horst. The force pushed Horst back aginst the car, and the gun slipped out of his hand by the car wheel. The two began grappling to reach the gun. Matt grabbed Horst by his hair, and pulled his head forward. He then pushed it back hard against the car's fender. The collision stunned Horst and he slid down to the ground.

Christine started getting to her feet, apparently all right. Matt could see someone moving caustiously down the driveway with a gun in his hand. In the distance he could here police sirens.

"Herr Garweiler," said Christine.

"What the hell is going on here?" responded Garweiler, holding the gun out in front of him.

"It's all right. We're not armed." Matt held out his arms in an open gesture.

Garweiler looked around and lowered the gun. When he saw Andre LeFevre's body, he gasped.

"We have something very important to show you regarding LeFevre & Cie. May we come into your chalet."

CHAPTER FORTY EIGHT

Monday, Washington's Birthday, was one of the rare three day weekends that members of the New York Stock Exchange get during the course of the year. Jack McGrory, having been persuaded by his wife to take the cold sea air at their Southampton house, was walking along the beach, ruminating. He was still feeling the deep gnawing sensation in his stomach. The next day would end forty highly profitable years of trading on the Stock Exchange. He was short two million shares of USOCO stock. Now with the apparent takeover by the Arabs, he would sure to be out of business by 10:00 AM the next morning, as his capital would be fully depleted by the uptick in the stock.

Well, thank God, he thought, he'd always paid cash for everything he owned. At least he would be able to keep his house and apartment. And there was enough money in the bank to pay the bills. But he was going to lose the firm. His father will be rolling over in his grave. Jack stared at the sea but his eyes were not focusing at the expanse of gray water. He only saw the vision of his business slipping away from him.

"Jack, Jack." His wife's voice penetrated his consciousness. "It's time to go back to New York. The car is waiting." Jack wondered how his wife would take the news -- up until now her only knowledge of finance was writing checks and saying 'charge-it' at Saks.

Jack turned towards her with sad eyes and calmly followed her instructions.

"I'll be right up," he said, walking up the sand to the entrance of his Tudor beach home. Jack and his wife gathered up their overnight bags and got in the limousine.

"Henry," said Jack to the chauffeur, "let's stop for the paper and a coffee at Silver's." Silver's was Southampton's most outrageously priced delicatessen, but the coffee was gourmet roast. Henry ran into the store and picked up the New York Post and two regulars to go. Jack wanted an excuse not to have to make small talk with his wife for the duration of the trip back into Manhattan.

Jack turned immediately to the business section, which comprises only one page in the tabloid format Post. Because of the long holiday weekend, there was little news of interest. Jack sighed. As the limo hit a large bump on the Long Island Expressway, Jack's eyes jumped to the bottom left hand page. There was an article dateline Geneva, UPI, with the following headline: Swiss Banker Murdered, Bank Closed After Irregularities Found.

The article went on to say that Andre LeFevre, 46, Managing Director of LeFevre& Cie, Geneva, was shot to death Saturday near his ski chalet in Gstaad allegedly by German banker, Horst Meyer, after a dispute. In a bizarre series of events, the Swiss bank authorities have closed the bank and frozen all assets pending charges of embezzlement against the dead banker and his assistant, Raoul Hengler.

The article further commented that late last week, it was announced that LeFevre & Cie, acting for Arab interests, planned a takeover of United States Oil Company, USOCO. These plans apparently now in disarray, and speculation among knowledgeable Swiss financiers indicate that Arab interests in fact did not exist, and that the embezzled funds were behind much of the run up in the USOCO stock.

Jack read the article over and over in disbelief. If it were true, the price of USOCO stock would tumble. Speculators, investors and traders would all be scambling to get out of their positions as USOCO's bubble began to burst. For Jack, this was the best news in the world. His two million share short position, instead of being the cause of his business's demise, would make this his most profitable trade ever.

"Goddamn," he said. "Better lucky than smart."

"What's that, dear?" said his wife.

"Nothing, Sweets, nothing at all."

CHAPTER FORTY NINE

Tuesday morning the floor of the Stock Exchange around Jack McGrory's post was the scene of complete and utter pandemonium. The investment community woke that day to digest further details in the Wall Street Journal about the death of Andre LeFevre, his embezzlement and theft of customer's funds used to finance the speculative attempt to greenmail the United State Oil Corporation. According to the report, the purpose of the greenmail was to enable LeFevre to recoup years of failing investments made on behalf of his clients, and to perpetrate history's largest financial blackmail scheme. USOCO had released a statement to the press which supported the news from Switzerland.

Floor traders from all the brokerage firms were screaming at Jack, asking him to indicate at what price the USOCO stock would open. The mounds of sell tickets were overflowing the counter at Jack's post. The clerks were scrambling to figure out how many shares were being offered for sale 'at the market'. Few buyers were apparent, except for those willing to purchase at much lower prices.

"Shut up, you guys," screamed Jack back at them. "It's going to take a couple of hours to sort this out before we can start trading the stock." For Jack, this was a bonanza --it looked like the stock was going to open at least $20 dollars below Friday's close of $56 per share. That would mean that the two million shares sold short by him previously would be purchased to cover the short position at a profit of $40 million dollars.

"Not bad," thought Jack. Then he looked up at the worried brokers representing large long positions in USOCO that surrounded his post. "Aghh," he thought, "fuck'em if they can't take a joke."

Max Adler was sitting at his desk on top of which was a portable television screen. He was watching the Financial News Network, a cable television show that runs a delayed ticker tape across the bottom of the screen and offers live news coverage across the top. He was waiting for the report of the opening of the stock. Jimbo had estimated that his average purchase price of USOCO stock was about $45. The syndicate had purchased over a million and a half shares. Max's mind kept repeating over and over: make it open at $45, God please, make it open at $45.

The phone rang. Max did not pick it up -- he expected to be hearing from a lot of angry syndicate members. A few seconds later, his secretary buzzed and reported that Marty Fishbein was on the line. Max was surprised, but he knew the purpose of the call -- Marty wanted the last laugh. Max debated for a few seconds, then picked up the receiver.

"Yeah, Marty. What do you want?" Max tone was as gruff as he could make it.

"Max, Max. Don't be upset. I just called to thank you."

"Whaddaya mean?"

"You made me a lot of money in this USOCO stock. And you let me get out when I wanted to. Not every syndicate leader is that accommodating."

Max was silent for a moment. Was Marty sincere, or just rubbing salt into the wound, he wondered.

"What are you trying to say, Marty?"

"That as far as I'm concerned we are a great team. You tell me when to get into a stock, I'll tell you when to get out."

Max dropped the phone from his ear. Jesus, he thought, everyone's a goddam comedian.

"Marty, do you want to be on my syndicate list again? Is that what you're getting at?"

"Sure, Max. Give me a call the next time you have something going. I'll give you my opinion then."

"No hard feelings."

"Nahh. None at all." Suddenly, Max could hear raucous laughter coming from the other end of the phone.

"Shit," he said out loud, but Marty was past hearing him. Max slammed down the phone.

His secretary put her head in his door and said that three other syndication members were waiting on different phone lines to talk to him. Which one, she asked, did he wish to speak to first.

By 11:30, the stock had still not opened. Nick Bianco sat behind his desk in the trading room watching the Quotron

242

machine. He held 500,000 shares of USOCO, purchased at an average price of $55. Through some of his trading in the stock he had managed to make a $3 million profit. Yet if the stock dropped more than 6 points, his profit would be gone. Nick assessed his chances of coming out even. Nick checked his watch, a heavy gold affair that left marks on his arm. One and a half hours after the Exchange's opening bell, the stock had still not opened. A muscle tightened in Nick's stomach. It was going to be bad.

From the corner of his eye he saw his boss approach the desk. Nick tried to avert his eyes, as if not looking might make his boss go off elsewhere. It was harldly a successful ploy.

"Did the stock open yet?"

"No, not yet."

"See me in my office after it does."

"Right."

His boss walked away and Nick turned his head back to the Quotron machine. The cursor near the USOCO stock listing began to blink. Then the price began to change. $35. Nick was temporarily stunned. The loss, with the three million dollar gain would amount to $7 million. A flush began to cover his whole body. He suddenly felt as though he could not get any oxygen into his lungs, as if the room were devoid of air. He started to move in the direction of the men's room. By the time he reached the next desk where the gold traders sat, he was violently sweating.

He spent the next fifteen minutes in the men's room wiping his face with cold paper towels. Then he went to his boss's office. Ten minutes later he emerged, went to his desk, opened his rarely used attache case, and started emptying the personal items from his desk into it, saying nothing to his assitants. As he left the room, he casually waved his hand and said 'see'ya' to a staring group.

He got in a cab and went to Carol's apartment. He opened the door with his own key. She was not there. Probably out shopping, thought Nick. He lay down on the couch to wait for her, and fell instantly to sleep.

She woke him when she returned three hours later.

"What are you doing here? Why didn't you call?"

Nick sat upright on the couch trying to think of a way to explain. "I'm here because I'm a free man now. I'm retiring."

Carol knew better. "You were fired," she said.

"Nahh. I resigned. They don't give you any freedom there. I'm going to start my own company."

"Do you have the money to do that?"

"Yeah. I've got money. Then I'm going to get a divorce and marry you." Nick's own plans were beginning to make him excited.

"How much money do you have?" Carol was more concerned about her own welfare than his.

"Enough, enough. I've got plenty. Plenty." He was beginning to get horny. "Hey, I didn't come here to talk." He started fondling her.

"Sure, Nick." Carol had once heard him say that his monthly payments were killing him. She suspected that there was little put aside for new companies. "But first, honey, you know, I'm a little tight for money right now. Could you give me another hundred?"

"No problem. Shit. You really think that there's a problem. You'll get it. Now let's fuck."

Carol looked at his eyes. "After you write out the check."

"Bitch," he said. "Mother fucking bitch." He put on his coat and walked out the door.

Having returned home late Monday evening, Smathers had not seen any news regarding the debacle until Tuesday morning. He had arrived early at his desk, opened his cup of take-out coffee, taken a gulp and unfolded the Journal to the front page. The news headline had caused him such a jolt that he spit out his coffee all over the newspaper on his desk.

He did not call Nick. He did not want to let on to Nick that there might be a problem concerning USOCO and himself. He put in a call to Owen Perry at USOCO's headquarters but no one answered at that early hour. Besides, he realized that he would not really have anything to ask, except a confirmation of what already was before him in the newspaper. He then dialled Betsy.

"Uh, Bets, have the broker sell out the, eh, you know account." Smathers always had the constant fear that his phone calls were being monitored.

"Why? I thought we were going to hold onto everything for a while. At least that's how you sounded over the weekend."

"Uh, well, things are changing. Just call and leave the order with him. Before the market opens. Okay, honey." Betsy sensed that something was not quite right -- his tone was unusually solicitious.

Fifteen minutes later, Betsy was back on the phone with Smathers.

"Jon, what's going on with this stock? The broker laughed when I said to sell."

"Uh, I don't know yet. Everything's a little up in the air now."

"What do you mean 'up in the air'?"

"Unclear. Unsettled. Don't worry. Things will work out."

"You liar. Things will not work out. The broker already told me that the options were as good as dead. And you know it as well as he does."

"No, Betsy, don't get upset. We'll get our money out. Just not as much."

"I had $10,000 in there with you. I listened to you. Even when I wanted to sell, I still listened to you. So you better be right when you say my $10,000 is still there."

"Jeez, Bets, calm down. We're partners. We're in this together."

"Now we're partners. Before I had nothing I was

allowed to say. Just Bets do this and Bets do that. But when things look bad suddenly we're partners. Well, I sure hope that things are not as bad as they look -- because if they are, I'll, I'll.." Betsy clearly had no idea what she would do -- so to cover herself she instead slammed down the phone.

At the market's opening, Smathers went out to the reception area at the other end of the building where a Quotron machine was made available for visitors, and plugged in the USOCO symbol. As he had expected, the machine repsonded by saying that the stock had not yet opened. Smathers returned to his desk and began the wait. He attempted to do work, but his mind was in a state of no function. He took routine phone calls and pushed some memos around. Colleagues dropped in to discuss the USOCO affair, but Smathers showed no intrest in responding to them. Every fifteen minutes he returned to the machine. The longer the wait, the worse he knew it would be. For an investor, such periods are a form of agony.

At 11:40 AM he went out to the machine again and pulled up the stock price. This time it registered $35. Smathers put in different symbols and got the quote on the options he held. Instead of the anticipated $8 per share, it read 1/16th, or 6.25 cents. Samthers had paid a $1 each -- on the $50,000 he invested, he would receive $3,125 back. He was close to tears.

He went back to his office and debated taking the rest of the day off. The phone rang -- it was Betsy.

"I know everything. The broker finally explained it all. You've lost all your money. And mine too."

"I'll pay you back."

"You knew this morning, but you still strung me along."

Smathers started to shake his head. "I didn't know," he protested. "But I admit it didn't look good."

"It doesn't look good for a lot of things."

"Like what else?"

"Like our marriage."

Smathers closed his eyes and grimaced. He ran his fingers through his hair. He had put her off for so many years, but somehow it never occurred to him that she wouldn't always be there waiting for him.

"I'm still working. That's not a problem. We can still get married."

"Yes, we can." said Betsy softly. "But not to each other."

The phone's ring moments later jarred Smathers out of his stupor.

"Uh. This is John Wortz at the Securities and Exchange Commission. It appears that your name was mentioned as a broker-reference with regards to the account of a certain Betsy Caldwell. We have been reviewing her transactions and are concerned with its unusual volume with regards to USOCO options. Could we meet with you to discuss the matter and your relationship, if any, with this account?"

Smathers closed his eyes. Fuck me, he thought.

CHAPTER FIFTY

March, 1986

Matt, Whitey and Christine sat around a small wooden table in the tap room of the New York Yacht Club. Located in the heart of mid-town New York, it was essentially a weekday club -- it was actually closed during the weekend when most of its members were out sailing. It is among the most prestigious of sailing clubs in North America -- its main room is filled, museum like, with half and full models of the famous racing and cruising boats that its members owned. One table in the center of a room was conspicuous by its emptiness -- it was where the America's Cup had been for so many years prior to having been won away by the Australians.

Whitey had been watching Matt and Christine with some interest. He had invited them to his club to celebrate her visit to New York. He noticed that Matt barely took his eyes off her, which, Whitey sensed, Christine was most aware of. Christine was staying at Matt's apartment -- Matt had taken the last two days off, since her arrival, to help her 'settle in'. Whitey was very amused with that -- how much 'settling' could she need?

"What finally happened to Raoul?" asked Whitey. "Is he in the slammer?"

"No, he's in jail," answered Christine, evidently unaware of what 'slammer' meant. Whitey and Matt laughed.

"It's not funny," she added, only slightly annoyed. "In fact, it's very sad. Andre LeFevre's dead, Raoul's in jail, and Horst's out on bail awaiting trial for the murder of Andre."

"We're going to testify in his defense," added Matt. "After all, Andre did have a gun on all of us. He stands a good chance to get off on self-defense."

"Then what will he do -- can he go back to his father's bank?"

"He's already back," said Matt. "His father was so stunned by the news that he had a heart attack. Someone has to manage the bank."

"And what about you, Christine? What are you going to do now that LeFevre is closed."

"I cannot do anything there. Everyone knows that I was the one who uncovered the mess at LeFevre. So while everyone thinks I'm wonderful, no one wants to hire me because they think I will do the same thing at their office."

"That's terrible."

"Yes and no. I did not want to be a secretary any more anyway. This gives me an excuse."

"How long are you planning on staying?" asked Whitey, already knowing from Matt that she had indefinite plans.

"Well." She smiled coyly at Matt. "I guess that depends."

"Depends on what?"

"On when I get an answer." With anyone else, Whitey would have been annoyed with this game, but somehow Christine's demeanor lifted it to very charming.

"Okay," said Whitey. "I'll bite. Answer from whom."

"New York University. I've applied to go there. For a degree in business. An MBA, as you call it."

Whitey was sincerely impressed. "I didn't know you had a bachelor's degree."

"I do. A degree in Economics which I got in Switzerland. But it was useless to me there -- I'm not smart enough to be a professor, and they didn't hire women for management jobs. After I finish school here, I hope to stay in New York and work."

Whitey could see Matt's face beaming.

"Christine is very smart," Matt added. "She should get a degree on the spot."

Whitey looked at Christine. "I couldn't agree more. In fact, after all that you did in Geneva it has been clearly proven you have the two most important ingredients for the making of a brilliant Wall Street tycoon." Whitey waved the waiter over. "Do you have any large pieces of paper lying around."

The waiter, a veteran of the club and used to odd requests from members who often designed ships' hulls on the restuarant's linen napkins, shrugged his shoulders and schuffled off to the bar area. He returned with a piece of white cardboard similar to those found in shirts returned from commerical laundries. "Will this do?" he said, as he brought it over.

"Perfect," said Whitey. He pulled out a felt tip pen and began to print in large letters:

WE HEREBY PRESENT TO

CHRISTINE EVINS

AN HONORARY DEGREE IN

BUSINESS ADMINSTRATION

IN RECOGNITION OF HER INNATE ABILITY

TO BE BOTH LUCKY AND SMART

AT THE SAME TIME

Signed, WALL STREET

ORDER ADDITIONAL COPIES NOW

Additional copies of
GREENMAIL
may be ordered for $5.95 each
plus $1.00 per book for handling and postage.

Please send your check to:

BIXTER BOOKS
250 EAST 63RD ST.
SUITE 1203
NEW YORK, NY 10021
(212) 888-1693

Mr/Mrs/Ms _____

Address _____

City_____State_____Zip _____

No. of Copies_____Amount Enclosed $_____